To Lucy

my favourite elf !

Benji

Tons of love x x x x .

BENJI MING

DB PUBLISHING

First published 2016 by DB Publishing, an imprint of JMD Media Ltd,
Nottingham, United Kingdom.

ISBN 978-1-78091-542-5

Printed in the UK

1

The gravel crunched ostentatiously and satisfyingly as Derek eased the blue Toyota Avensis up the winding, tree-lined drive of the former stately home, now a country house hotel/conference centre. His innate socialism naturally revolted against the corporate hospitality event they were about to take part in, but it was their bread-and-butter activity, and thespian beggars cannot be choosers, can they? So he prepared to kowtow and scrape as much as necessary for the success of the event. The casual observer would be forgiven for thinking he actually enjoyed the process, so good was he at it.

Phaedra had long since jettisoned any political pretensions; years of getting her knockers out in 'Boobs Not Bombs' protests had not altered government policy one iota, surprisingly enough. Although they had been the fourth most viewed pair of breasts on the Internet for a few glorious weeks, slightly tempered by the fact that number two was Judy Finnegan, and number three a Japanese sumo wrestler. She could not remember who or what number one had been. Now just earning some sort of living in the performing/acting field was the limit of her ambitions. She still enjoyed the murder mysteries, however: you usually got a meal out of it, a drink if you were lucky, sometimes even a bit of flirtation. And the pay wasn't bad. But they were much more fun in the old days, before Derek staged a coup and took over the company. Now he micromanaged all the actors, giving them very little leeway for their own judgement and improvisation; when Caroline, Paul, Arthur, Henrietta, Barry, et cetera were part of the team, vast hilarity usually ensued, often drunkenness, and sometimes even wine theft. Ah, the old days.

And ah!; Barry. Phaedra still thought of him, with a mixture of regret, guilt, affection and annoyance. If only he had not been so jealous, things might have gone better; if only she had not given him good reason to be jealous, things might also have gone better. But could that level of passion have lasted beyond a year, jealousy or no? And then there was that horrible aftermath, still working together for years, though not officially being together, but kind of…she shuddered to think about the mutual abuse and recriminations they got involved in, till Barry eventually threw in the towel and went off to be a tree surgeon in Sweden. He always liked to make a theatrical entrance or exit, and that certainly was one.

Derek managed to get them a 'syndicate room', whatever that meant, to change in. Did not always happen; toilets and corridors were not unknown. And as they were ludicrously early, as always (another Derekian innovation), their leader magnanimously allowed them to have a tea or coffee. At their own expense, of course. Tonight it was 'Office Murder', one of their most performed plots, and one Phaedra knew off by heart, as did the other performers: Peg, Peter C. and Tom. Derek would still insist on going through the whole thing beforehand however, relishing any slight mistake by the cast. It was all so trying, especially as the newer actors insisted on doing this bit in character, and being stupidly enthusiastic about the whole farcical business. *Am I getting jaded?* she thought; *no, just efficiently professional*, she answered herself, possibly disingenuously.

***

Three hours later and they were back in the syndicate room, first gig of the Christmas season successfully behind them; though Phaedra thought Tom, as Inspector, could not hold a candle to Barry's former effusive expositions. He used to command the room at this point, the denouement; it was his moment in the spotlight. He *was* The Inspector, and everyone hung on his words, trying to work out if their answer was right or not. Usually, as 'Inspector Boireau', Barry would not name the culprit till the very end of his explanation, keeping them all guessing, building up to a crescendo on his very last word: the villain's name. Tom was not so theatrical, though much more camp. It was a corporate gig, for whom she never asked; it was a Monday, December 8; and the participants had been generally middle-aged, so pissedness had not been a problem, as it could sometimes be on company Christmas dos. Especially if the social secretary had not told her colleagues what she had arranged, and most just saw it as an inconvenience, delaying them getting off with each other. But tonight had been OK, the punters were fairly intelligent for once, had asked the right questions, and seemed to be interested most of the time. She had managed to get a vegetarian meal, ate it all, and swigged as much wine as she could whenever Derek was elsewhere engaged. Almost all the teams had guessed the murderer correctly, largely due to Derek going round and pretty much telling them while they were coming up with their solutions; something he had started doing recently. It might be nice for them, but it made giving a first prize bloody difficult.

But that was not her problem, she thought as she changed, catching Derek sneaking a quick look at her in knickers and bra. What a bloody hypocrite the man was: he used to tell Barry off for that sort of thing. At least Barry was honest about it, and Phaedra did not mind been ogled by men; or women, for that matter. 'Did you hear about Colin?' he suddenly asked, reddening slightly, probably to cover up for having been rumbled. 'What about him?' Peter C. replied, openly ogling both girls. But he was Derek's friend, therefore allowed to. 'Found dead in his grotto on Saturday afternoon – first day of his Santa stint.' 'What?' exploded everyone, apart from Tom, who did not know Colin. 'Where? How? How do you know?' Derek explained he had heard it on the local radio on Sunday morning, last item on the news; then it had slipped out completely when some celebrity gossip hit the airwaves. 'In Watford, at one of the malls, where he always does it. They are treating it as suspicious.' 'Disgruntled kid – didn't get what he wanted!'

'More like disgruntled parent these days – they probably had to pay to see him.' 'Disgruntled Elf, knowing Colin!'

'Well at least with Colin it wouldn't be for kiddie-fiddling.'

Each actor had their response; all except Tom had worked with Col at some point. He was a fairly popular character, though known to be a bit of a boozer, given the chance. Which was a good point in Phaedra's eyes. Didn't work with them much nowadays, probably due to Derek's new regime. (He was of course responsible for hiring the actors.)

'Bloody hell! Poor Colin. He must've only been about, what, forty-five? Fifty?' This from Peter C. 'Why was it suspicious?'

'Didn't hear it properly,' (Derek), 'something about his head in his sack? Must be something about it in the papers, or Internet.' Phaedra was not particularly friendly with Colin; had not seen him for years, in fact. But it did dampen the atmosphere in the car on the way home. He was one of the typical murder mystery/corporate entertainment performers she came across: probably started out aspiring to play The Dane one day, or similar, but instead slipped into this shadowy world on the periphery of Real Acting, where people like them lived. They all knew each other, worked for various murder mystery companies, mostly based in London, and at exhibitions, product launch parties, walkabout characters, the odd panto, Santa, et cetera. Some still aspired to some kind of success someday, others had slid slowly into middle age without realising it, until one day they discovered they were officially too old to be an aspiring young actor, and touring theatre companies no longer wanted them. Derek was the former, Peter C. the latter; she was not sure about Tom, and suspected Peg still harboured hopes of stardom.

And herself? Still in her thirties, there was some hope, but she was not a conventional beauty, as most moderately successful actresses were. You had to be brilliant to be ugly and successful; even Victoria Wood had resorted to plastic surgery, and she was brilliant, and had never been ugly. Her light blue eyes were too big, she had always been told; often unkindly by other children. Luckily she had not developed a complex about it, or gone down the cosmetic surgery route herself. Not that she could ever have afforded it; but a philanthropic aunt had once offered to pay for it, should it aid her fledgling acting career. Her hair was very blond, naturally, and her lips what could be described as 'voluptuous', in common with the rest of her body; occasionally veering towards the 'chubby'. Or perhaps 'big boned'? A pathetic claim by fat people, she had always thought.

She had had her moments, of course: her one-woman show at the Edinburgh Festival (Fringe), for instance. But the last decade had mostly been spent doing this kind of thing, having to make a living out of it, however irregular. She suspected Colin had been the same, just 10 years older. She did not know if he had been married, had kids, girlfriend, et cetera; she suspected not. Most of his type were at heart sad, lonely failures. Just like her, she sighed, as the Avensis made its way south towards the metropolis, Derek playing his horrible Bob Dylan to avoid a conversation he might not be able to control.

2

Terence nervously fingered his ticket as the train drew into Nottingham Station. It was both nervousness and excited anticipation; he was buoyed by yesterday's success, and looked forward to a repeat performance. But there was always the chance things could go wrong: so many variables involved. And he had a great task to fulfil.

He caught sight of his reflection in the train window as he stood up to leave his seat: tall, skinny, gawky, bespectacled, bit spotty, the archetypal geek. In some Hollywood romcoms he might be the unlikely romantic hero, winning the girl with his oddball charm; but not here. Terence had long since stopped caring about his appearance, not that he ever did much. Such ephemeral concerns were beneath him; he could not begin to understand how anyone could possibly be interested in things like fashion, pop music or sport. His life might have been different had his appearance been; but he was now set on the path he intended to follow.

He partly blamed his parents, partly thanked them, for making him who he was. They were of course a bit worried about him; but not enough. He was still young, only 21; plenty of time to sort his life out and decide what he wanted to do. And apparently lots of 'kids' his age spent huge amounts of time in their bedrooms, 'gaming', or on the Internet, and did not appear to have many friends in the real world; so our Ter was not so different, was he? Well, only in degree: he had *no* real friends, and precious few virtual. That used to upset Terence, immensely; but even that was behind him now. His Quest was all-consuming.

He had already ascertained the quickest route to the House of Fraser department store, Nottingham's biggest, and promptly made his way there. The sights of the city were of no interest to him, despite never having visited before. As a boy he might have been attracted by the Robin Hood connections, or where the evil Sheriff hung out; but not now. He entered the building a few minutes before 1.00, as planned, making his way up the escalators to the top floor. Terence knew the virtues of anonymity, and kept as unobtrusive as possible, walking purposefully and not making eye contact with anyone. It was not time to be caught yet, if at all.

And then he was there: Santa's Area. In these ultra-sensitive-to-child-protection days, grottos were out in most shops; the Bearded One had to be in full view, making Inappropriate Behaviour very difficult. Even with his Elves, if costs stretched that far. Usually they didn't. Here, the Kindest Man in the World sat on a golden throne in a corner of the Children's Clothing department, with no helpers at all. There were a couple of reasonably decorated Christmas trees, two tubs full of presents (for older or younger kids respectively), and a low velvet stool to interview those lucky children on. Sitting on Santa's knee is completely out of the question nowadays; touching in any way is contrary to official policy. But if a baby is thrust into Father Christmas's arms for a photo, sensible discretion is usually in order. This particular incarnation of St Nicholas was Geoff Nicholson, not an aspiring actor this time, but a respectable member of the Nottingham Round Table, who used his genuine white beard and hair to earn an extra bit of cash at this time of year, as he had for many years now. Plus, he genuinely liked children, and enjoyed the whole Christmas experience. Terence approved of the hair and beard, it made the whole illusion a little more believable; but the costume was tacky and dirty, no attention to detail. How could kids be taken in? And where was the man's professional pride? At the moment he seemed more interested in chatting up the pretty young female shop assistants; they always had a soft spot for Santa. Terence could forgive him that, if not empathise.

Terence watched for a few seconds from behind a rail of fairy dresses, waiting for his moment to strike, like a crouching tiger. Albeit skinnier and more gawky. In fact, not much like a tiger at all. But he could not leave it too long, or he might be noticed; he did not look like the normal shopper in that area of the store, and knew it. He also knew that Geoff had his half hour lunch break spot on 1.00; he was a creature of habit, as most people are. It is surprising the information people put on their computers, readily hacked by an expert like Terence. Sure enough, before Terence could get uncomfortable, Geoff took out his 'Feeding reindeer – back at 1.30' sign, stood up, put it on his vacated chair, and began to waddle towards the staff canteen.

'How's it going then, mate? Kids been behaving themselves?'

Terence sidled up to the departing legend. Geoff could not remember having spoken to this skinny, spotty youth before, but everyone in the store felt they had the right to speak to Santa, and generally did. Terence had carefully dressed similarly to the House of Fraser staff, which to be honest was not hard – the ubiquitous black – so the mythical philanthropist could be forgiven for assuming he was a fellow employee. Terence himself hated this informal 'matey' style of conversation – in fact, he hated most sorts of conversation – but could pull it off when needs required. He could have been a brilliant actor, under different circumstances. The unlikely pair wandered towards the staff canteen chatting, looking like Laurel and Hardy.

'Ever worked in Lapland? I hear lots of British Santas go there,' Terence asked nonchalantly, when they were halfway across the shop floor.

'Yeah, did it a few times,' Geoff replied with a chuckle, though not a full-throated 'Ho-ho-ho'. 'It was a laugh. Bloody cold though! That was about ten years ago; haven't done it recently. Just do the occasional charity appearance apart from this.'

Geoff Nicholson had just, unwittingly, sealed his fate.

'Got to go for a piss, pal,' Mr Claus helpfully informed Terence as they left the shop floor.

'Oh, me too,' the skinny one replied, holding the door open for the fat one. Relief; the men's room was empty. Terence's plan was nearer fulfilment. Geoff did not have the natural Santa-esque girth so he used padding, merely a pillow today, making the process of urination in the urinal a fairly complicated one, requiring both hands. Even more helpful for Terence. He pretended to pee in a nearby trough, again helped by the fact that men do not look elsewhere than their own bits when peeing, for fear of homosexual allegations. After a few seconds he walked up behind the red-garbed colossus, as if going to wash his hands; then suddenly, violently, viciously, slammed Geoff's head against the tiled wall in front of him, with as much force as he could muster.

There was a sickening crack as flesh and bone collided with ceramic tiles; Geoff did not even grunt before losing consciousness and sliding to the floor, willy still hanging out and dribbling over his red vestments. That blow would probably have killed him anyway, but Terence wanted to make sure, and if possible do it in an appropriate way. Blood poured from the head wound as he pulled out Santa's false belly and stuffed as much as he could into Geoff's mouth, finishing the job off by suffocation. He was careful to shield the body from anyone coming in at the door; he could get away with pretending to be helping the stricken Santa who had just slipped and hit his head on the wall should anyone enter. But luck was with Terence: no one did, and he was able to drag the body into a cubicle and wipe the blood off the floor and wall with a paper towel before washing his hands and quickly exiting the staff area. He knew he had not covered his tracks completely, but there was nothing obvious to the casual loo visitor, and he would be well away by the time the ex-Santa was discovered. Terence had left as much of the padding in Geoff's mouth as he could, to satisfy his inclination to make the punishment fit the crime; and the open fly and protruding penis might point investigators in the direction of an unfortunate sexual adventure, rather than the real motive.

A young lad entered the gents as Terence left; job done just in time. He had his headphones on and appeared to be absorbed in whatever rubbish he was listening to, so Terence thought there was little chance that he would be remembered. He resisted the temptation to alter the 'Feeding reindeer' sign, left the premises quickly but unhurriedly, and sauntered back to the station. Relief and elation flooded his body; this was living! Two down, and how the bastards deserved it. He could now understand bloodlust, and empathised with tyrants like Vlad the Impaler and Pol Pot. But what *he* was doing was justified, of that he was certain. Terence deliberately looked at his reflection in the train window this time: you may look gawky and geeky, son, but you have the power of life or death over Santas! And this was only the beginning.

3

Barry slowly let himself down on his rope from the huge spruce tree he had been gradually felling. Generally he just felled the trees, rather than surgically reduced them; much more satisfying. He still said 'Timber!', even if under his breath, when a forest giant hit the deck. But this one was too near someone's forest log cabin, their summer country retreat, to be safely chopped at ground level; and it was leaning slightly the wrong way, endangering the boreal bungalow should his calculations be a bit awry. So he had had to laboriously climb his way up, using his old but trusty spikes and a strop (tough fabric strap attached to his harness and wrapped round the tree trunk) to secure himself. He had a fairly good head for heights, but always felt a bit nervous at the top of a big mutha, especially when the branches had been stripped away and he was secured only by what looked like a glorified matchstick. He knew the anchor point was as safe without the surrounding branches as with; it just looked less so, 'more exposed' as mountaineers would say. So it was with a smidgeon of relief that his feet touched the ground again.

It was a very cold day in the forests of Sweden; it was probably a very cold day in the cities and fields of Sweden too. But the forests were in the majority when it came to the land mass. This had made climbing and chogging (reducing the height of the tree bit by bit, from the top) all the more difficult, with layers of bulky warm clothes to contend with, especially the chainsaw gloves. But days were very short at this time of year, Barry reflected, so he was being paid for the hardship rather than the hours. The temperature was probably hovering around -5C, if temperature does indeed hover, so gloves had to be kept on at all times. His pal Sven (yes, really! It had always amused Barry) had just called him down for lunch, and Barry lost no time in throwing off his safety harness and extraneous gear before heading for the relative warmth of the van, parked nearby. There was a thick covering of snow, and the lovely smell of pine in the air, tempered with the odour of chainsaw oil, made a slightly sickly combination. The pine made him think of Christmas, the oil of…well, chainsaws. Work.

Work was what kept Barry going. It was all he did, in fact. He had been in Sweden for five years now, and had never been to a Swedish cinema. Or a sauna, about which the Swedes are very keen. Not even those sort. He went out drinking with the lads, something else the Swedes were very keen on; but had never had a girlfriend, never visited Stockholm or one of the other cities, and had not even been skiing, something *he* had been keen on as a boy in Scotland. He just worked, usually with Sven, occasionally others, and in his spare time went on long walks through the forests, animal-spotting and pondering. He had learnt the language pretty well, despite most Swedes speaking English; apart from the accent, Sven was almost perfect. He rented a tiny apartment in Ytterrhogdal, a village in the middle of the country, close to most of his work; he kept himself to himself most of the time, said 'Hej!' to his neighbours, and never got outrageously pissed. Sven, much younger than Barry, thought he must be hiding some secret passion, or suffering from depression. In a way he was right on both counts.

Sven was already sitting in the front of the van, heater on to give them some warmth. 'Brass monkeys, eh Barry?' he smirked as Barry climbed into the other seat. Sven loved to show off his command of English idiom. 'But why are the monkeys brass, and what are they doing out in weather like this? I thought you English were a nation of animal lovers.' 'British,' Barry corrected; like most foreigners, Sven could not grasp the constitutional make-up of the United Kingdom. He then filled Sven in on the supposed Naval origin of the phrase, which Sven thoughtfully mulled over as he chewed his beef sandwich, on rye bread. Barry had cheese in his sandwiches; Herrgardsost, a local speciality. He always liked to buy local if he could. He was trying to read a Swedish novel, *Livlakarens Besok* by Per Olov Enquist; about halfway through, he understood it pretty well, if not finding it gripping. Sven read the sports pages of *Aftonbladet*, a Swedish tabloid; Rix FM, a local music station, played on the van's radio.

'Javla helvete!' Sven suddenly expostulated (a minor Swedish oath). 'Did you hear that?'

'No, what are you on about?' Barry replied, surprised by his normally phlegmatic friend's unusual agitation.

'It said three Santa Clauses have mysteriously died in England' (he meant Britain) 'in the last few days! They think it might be a serial Santa slayer!'

Sven seemed very amused by this; the Swedish sense of humour was something Barry had still to get to the bottom of. Sven was so good at English he even liked a bit of alliteration, even if he did not know the word for it, and 'serial Santa slaying' appealed to him, especially with the appropriate double meaning of 'sleigh/slay' thrown in. Barry was interested, but only slightly; it was probably a media exaggeration, and one magnified by distance.

'Oh, I did that once,' he told his Scandinavian chum, 'in fact three Christmases in a row, to be more accurate. I quite enjoyed it, the kids were fun. Most of the time. Though one gypsy kid pulled my beard down in Debenhams, it was on elastic, and slowly made its way back up my face, in front of the next set of kids waiting to see me. They looked horrified. Probably ruined their childhood there and then.' That tickled the Swedish surgeon's funny bone even more, and he collapsed in a paroxysm of laughter. 'You English are so funny!' he finally managed to get out ('British!' – Barry). 'Especially you, Berry,' (Sven's clever play on words). 'I am surprised you don't have a chick, Swedish girls like men who make them laugh!'

This was now getting into uncomfortable conversation territory for Barry, especially with the younger man, who could not be expected to understand the deep-seated and traumatic reasons for his chick-less existence. He did not want to be thought of as gay – because he wasn't; but he had no desire to try to explain to his friend all the trauma he had gone through with P., and his reasons for fleeing to the backwoods of

Sweden. So a quick look at his watch and 'We'd better get back to it, I suppose' nipped that awkward conversation in the bud. Another tree reference, Sven.

They plodded back to the railway line between Karlstad and Ostersund and carried on, felling everything within five metres of the line. Mostly spruce, with a scattering of birch. It was getting colder now, the sun low in the southern sky, the railway stretching away on a straight line to infinity, bounded by the otherwise boundless snow-clad pine forests on either side. Never was perspective so obviously demonstrated. The ear protectors and roar of the chainsaws prevented conversation, even when they were near each other, which was not often, to lessen the chances of being accidentally squashed by someone else's felled tree. Trains were a rare relief. This was how Barry liked it; too noisy and busy to think about other things. Misery is a luxury of the lazy, he hypothesised.

But the mention of the Santas had of course wobbled his protective audio bubble, and as he cut into yielding tree flesh he could not help thinking of his times as the ubiquitous present-giver, especially his one 'season' in Lapland, in arctic Finland. When was that – the year of Phaedra – 2004, 10 years ago! God, was it that long ago? Horrible to think it was. And had he really moved on? Surely he must have, in all that time. But he was not the same man now as he had been then; now he was quieter, more introspective, less outgoing and show-offy. A lot less. Was that good? He had liked himself how he had been, and thought others did too; but did they really? Maybe only a particular type of person did; Ruth, his first big love before P., would have preferred the current Barry. But he was how he was, the results of circumstances and history. He thought he had got over his depression and breakdown, and that this duller Barry was the result. Or was it just maturity? Greater self-knowledge? God, it was hard to say. Much better not to think about it, and just get on with the job. He dug the screaming chainsaw into the innocent Norway Spruce with renewed vigour, the sawdust showering his protective trousers and surrounding virgin snow with arcs of wooden snowflakes.

4

Wednesday, 10 December, and Phaedra was on her way to another murder mystery, this time with only Tom and Derek. Another team was at a different event that evening, but she had drawn the short straw, as she saw it; she didn't particularly like either of her male colleagues. Did Derek do it deliberately, just to annoy her? He had tried it on with her once, several years ago, after the Barry thing was over. To his credit he had kept the relationship professional after her rejection of him, giving her as much work after as before; but he was often critical of her performances, pointing out every tiny mistake she made, and sometimes damning her with false praise. He also could not resist the opportunity to have a dig at Barry whenever he could, despite the fact that he had not worked for *Murder on the Menu* for several years, and was now in Sweden. Phaedra had always felt that Derek was jealous of Barry; her ex was much livelier and funnier, and in her eyes better looking. But each to his or her own. Derek was now happily remarried, and she and Barry, as far as she knew, single and lonely. The ways of Fate are not always fair, she mused.

'Did you hear another Santa's been found dead, in suspicious circumstances?' Derek suddenly piped up, clearly annoyed that the current conversation between Tom and Phaedra (celebrity gossip) was not under his control.

'No...where? When? How?' she tiredly replied, grudgingly abandoning the previous inane chat.

'Nottingham: House of Fraser, I think. Found in the staff loos, stomach padding stuffed in his mouth, and knob hanging out!'

'Well, it was the staff loos, that is to be expected.' (Tom)'Yeah, but accidentally suffocating on your own belly padding isn't so common, I believe.' (Phaedra)

'Bizarre sexual experiment? Like that Tory MP found dead in suspenders and an orange in his mouth a few years ago?' This from Tom, who enjoyed the odd bizarre sexual experiment himself.

'But he also had a cracked skull and huge wound to his forehead!' Derek trumped them all, satisfyingly.

'I'm still going with the sexual experiment,' Tom persisted, 'but his chum got cold feet and buggered off. But not literally.''Anyone we know?' Phaedra asked, vaguely interested.

'Don't think so,' Derek replied, 'I don't think he was an actor. Man of about sixty-five. Genuine hair and beard, they said. Heard it on the radio this morning. Apparently he was only found when the queue of kids and parents waiting to see him got so big that people started jumping it, and fighting ensued. Security had to hold scrapping mothers apart as they lashed out at each other with handbags, and kids stormed the present barrels! They had to clear the entire shop floor before they could search for Santa. He was only meant to be feeding his reindeer.' 'I bet they were good quality handbags at House of Fraser; plenty of solid brass buckles, could give a nasty bruise.' This from the bitchy Tom.

'Well, that's what they get for not employing a professional. More work for us next year,' was Phaedra's somewhat flippant response. The image of the flailing handbags overshadowed the true seriousness of the event in her mind.

Tonight's plot was 'Berkley's Bank', for a smaller group of punters, therefore fewer actors required.

Another Christmas do, another former country house hotel, this time near Bromsgrove. Phaedra enjoyed gigs at this time of year: these types of venue always made her feel Christmassy, with their tastefully decorated trees and the smell of wood smoke when you waltzed proprietorially through the big front doors. She had loved the festive season as a child, and those feelings had never quite left her, despite years of disappointments and dashed hopes. She still didn't know what she was doing for Christmas this year; she wanted to spend it with a loved one, but such a creature did not exist at the moment, and had not for some time. None of her sexual forays had been very successful since Barry, to be honest, male or female.

This time they changed in an upstairs bedroom; managements also felt more charitable at this time of year. And it meant they could use the complimentary coffee and tea – and biscuits! After the usual verbal run-through of the plot, under Derek's masterful ear, they started to get changed, Phaedra eschewing the modesty of the toilet. Her early actor training had taught her to jettison all shyness: getting your kit off in front of everyone was considered the norm, male and female together. Her role tonight was Mrs Barton the housekeeper, important at the start of the event, but peripheral thereafter. That was OK with Phaedra; it meant she could concentrate on eating and drinking, and let the boys flounce around being important and 'driving the plot forward'. *Is this a metaphor for my life?* she wondered, putting on her white pinnie and funny white thing girls in service used to wear on their heads.

Derek had magnanimously allowed the TV to be switched on, at Tom's request of course, and headlines were scrolling along the screen beneath the newsreader/interviewer.

'Wait a minute – what was that?' Tom suddenly ejaculated, pointing at the box.

'What?' a joint response.

'Hang on – it'll come round again,' Tom suggested, one hand keeping the false moustache on his top lip while the glue dried. The man loved moustaches.

They waited in suspended animation, and sure enough it did: 'Third Santa found dead, Glasgow.' 'Third?' three incredulous voices piped up, almost simultaneously.

'Turn it up,' commanded Derek, and Tom complied, with his one glueless hand. However, there was no actual report of the incident before they had to go and face their public, just that tantalising headline to mull over, and slightly distract them from their theatrical tours de force. Once in character amongst your adoring, or unadoring, public, most other things are forgotten, but in her quieter moments Phaedra did do a bit of mulling about the Santa deaths. As a Christmas fan you did not want things like that to happen, however much you thought there were too many Santas about these days, diluting the magic.

Again the gig went well, if anything better than the last one. It often did with smaller groups: everyone got more involved, and information was easier to disseminate. Though Phaedra still missed Barry's hugely theatrical reveals, as Inspector. In this plot everyone had a role to play, the guests having been informed of their characters beforehand. Good liaison between *Murder on the Menu* and the organiser of the event had hopefully cast the parts appropriately. Did not always happen, however; someone's idea of the best person to play Cindy the village transvestite might not sit quite so comfortably with Steve, the insecure assistant head of HR. It was often best leaving the actors to make that choice on the night, based on their years of experience in spotting show-offs. Characters were then given more personal information in envelopes delivered on the night, and if all went well it became a game played by the guests, lubricated by the actors, with additional objectives to merely solving the crime: making money (currency provided by the actors), acquiring and taking drugs (ditto, apart from the most enterprising guests), getting married (not generally supplied), et cetera. So, basically, the guests made their own entertainment, facilitated by the supposed actors. Solutions were offered by the guests after dessert, the correct one explained, villain unmasked (could even be one of the guests in this type of plot), prizes given for objectives achieved, fun had by all, actors leave to crescendo of applause and punters think they have had a great time and got value for money. Whereas they could easily have done it themselves with a little effort and imagination. That's all we are doing, thought Phaedra; helping them play games. Did I do three years at drama school for this?

The TV was put on again as they changed, and just before they left the item they were waiting for appeared, shortly before the end of the *Ten O'Clock News*. And what they saw and heard shocked them. The latest Santa to die on the job, as it were, was known to them: Harvey Trout, another ex-murder mysterion. Cause of death as yet unknown; found dead in his grotto, one of the few places still to have one. No sign of a struggle, but the white bobble on the end of his hat was in his mouth when one of his Elves discovered him. Again, helper Elves a rarity these days. The reporter said the police were not necessarily linking the deaths, they were several hundred miles apart, but it would be quite a coincidence if they were not. And all found with something Santa-esquely strange, involving sack, hat, bells and belly. Serial Santa-slaying was not mentioned in the item, it not being certain how they had all died; but that was of course what Phaedra and co. were thinking.

'Bloody hell! This is getting bloody serious. Who's going to be next? I bet a lot of Santas will hang up their beards now,' Phaedra opined as they left the hotel, slightly tipsy punters offering them thanks for the evening as they pushed their way through the revolving doors.

'Col and Harvey have been Santaing for ages now,' Derek mused. 'They both did it in Lapland too, I think.'

'Oh yeah? So did Barry,' Phaedra added, thought processes racing ahead of her words.

'So he did!' Derek interposed, as they all climbed back into the Toyota, a slight tone of triumph in his voice. 'Well, I don't think I would ever sink that low. Bit of a humiliation for a serious actor, don't you think, Phaedra? Good thing *Murder on the Menu* keeps us all from that awful fate!' Pause. 'That was just before you chucked him, wasn't it?'

Phaedra had neither the energy nor the willpower to argue with the smug wanker about the definition of 'chucked', so just mumbled some sort of assent.

'Yes, pity, I suppose. I thought you two were good together, if a little combustible sometimes,' the patronising git added, insincerity dripping off every word – apart from 'combustible'. That at least was true. Phaedra had to bite her lip hard to stop herself saying what she really thought of Derek – that would surely come someday, when she no longer relied on him for employment. But she was silent the rest of the way back to London, letting the two boys criticise films, plays and other actors, as if they were in a position to do so.

Bloody Lapland – that had been the final straw. Christmas 2004, 10 years ago now. Hard to believe it was that long ago. Why hadn't she gone and met Barry on that frozen lake at Kemijarvi, or whatever it was called, on Christmas Eve? It was the kind of romantic, impulsive thing he loved to do, and to be honest so did she. OK, he hadn't arranged for them to stay anywhere over Christmas, and it was of course sub-zero most of the time over there, and there was very little daylight; but they would surely have managed somehow! The uncertainty would have made it all the more exciting. And all that snow, pine trees, reindeer, even perhaps the Aurora Borealis – it could have been wonderful, especially if they had found somewhere with a big log fire and a thick carpet to snuggle up on. A log cabin perhaps. Barry had said the punters coming to see Santa stayed in just such an abode. Perhaps he had even booked one, just not told her, as a surprise?

It was all academic now, of course; at the last minute she had decided not to go, but had not had the heart to tell him. She had made a few efforts to phone him, but the signal was not very good over there, and she had left a message – but she knew she had not tried very hard, and had been scared to actually tell him. She would not have been able to explain her decision, there was no practical reason to cancel the arrangement, just a feeling that she was running to him all the time, and that it should be more equal. That's what her friend Ali had said – so was that the main reason she did not go, the influence of another? Barry had always said she was too influenced by other people's opinions, not enough her own woman. Or was it that she had snogged Richard at a party a few days before, felt guilty, but also felt she should not need to feel guilty, and got angry at Barry for making her feel like that? He was such a jealous man, she knew that. Many women would have loved the fact that he adored her, wanted her and her only, and would do anything for her; but it made her feel constricted and tied down. She was a bit of a hippy – well, to be honest a lot of a hippy – and in theory did not believe in monogamy and possessive relationships – though her past relationship history did not bear out the efficacy of that lifestyle. But the idea of running to Lapland – well, flying, to be pedantic – to be with Barry at Christmas was just too bourgeois for the feminist anarchist in Phaedra, so she had bottled out, leaving Barry confused, cold and abandoned on a frozen lake in Arctic Finland.

Plus he was 11 years older than her, so they were at different stages in their lives. He had had a lot of girlfriends over the years, some long-term, others not, but had never wanted to 'settle down' and maybe even have kids – till now. But that was not where Phaedra was at; still in her (late)

20s then, she had no intention of homemaking, let alone reproducing, though she thought she probably would at some point. At that time she was still thinking of West End, Hollywood, stardom – but only in politically relevant stuff, of course. Marriage and children would get in the way of that ambition, and lessen her lefty credentials. If only she had met Barry 10 years before! He would not have been at the homemaking stage by then, they could have had a short but passionate relationship, then moved on to other things, and maybe even remained friends. But the timing, like a lot of things in her life, had been wrong. Or was it like that for everyone, and they just made the best of it?

He had managed to get back on Boxing Day, she going to meet him at Gatwick with fear and trepidation, and huge dollops of guilt. He of course had been angry – no, furious – she had cried, a lot, he had eventually relented, but things were never the same. For years they lived in a state of semi-relationship, not officially being together but kind of, and of course everyone still thought they were, despite denials. The thing was, they still fancied each other, a lot, and that physical attraction often overrode the logical decision that they should split up and move on. But often she did not want to shag him, despite huge amounts of 'petting', he got angry and frustrated, she told herself she should not do that any more, it was not fair, but then could not resist a bit of physical affection, so he thought this time she had changed her mind – oh it was so awful! She shuddered to think of how they had made each other's life hell, for so long. If only sex had not reared its unnecessary head. But he had said she oozed it, which secretly pleased her, of course; but all she really wanted to do was cuddle! Early bad sexual experiences had left their scars. They had both gone to counselling eventually, she for longer than him, and both had had some sort of breakdown.

And then, suddenly, out of the grey (it was November), Barry announced that he was moving to Sweden, to become a tree surgeon. To say Phaedra was flabbergasted was not completely true; she knew he had been doing some work for his pal Phil, who ran a tree surgery company, but she had no idea he had decided to give up acting and change both profession and abode. He must have been thinking of it for some time however, because he told her he had already been to tree school and got the necessary qualifications in tree climbing, chainsaw maintenance, aerial rescue, et cetera. And the choice of Sweden was not a complete surprise: it contained the things he liked – coldness, mountains and forests. At least she thought it contained mountains; Norway did, she was sure of that. But to give up performing was tantamount to an admission of failure: Barry had always been the optimistic, one-day-I-will-make-it-big-you'll-see type. He was born to perform, a natural show-off, and in her eyes sometimes brilliant. If only the rest of the world would realise! But now he was giving it all up, his hopes, his dreams, his aspirations – all because of her. He claimed it was not, that he was not enjoying it any more, had realised what a shallow, meaningless business it all was, how tree surgery was real, manly work compared to these poncey actors, et cetera; she knew all that was true, but also knew he was leaving because of her, could not stand being in the same country as her any more. At one time he had talked of disappearing and joining the Foreign Legion, but did not want to kill anyone, and was not even sure if it still existed. This was the next best thing: killing trees instead of people, lost forever in the impenetrable forests of Sweden.

Derek and Tom prattled on in the front, now appraising Kenneth Branagh. Negatively, of course. But those twats didn't have a tenth of his talent! But what about her – did she have any either? And if so, how much? Should she keep on plugging away, hoping for inexorable progress towards some sort of professional recognition, or take her father's advice and get a real job if she hadn't 'made it' by the time she was 35? Too late for that now! Murder mysteries had a shelf life, of that she was sure; there were already less this Christmas than there had been last year. Maybe Barry had been right to change 'career' while he still could, and it was a positive step rather than an admission of failure? But deep down she did not think so; she knew he had given it all up because of her, and the guilt was always there. What a bastard, making her feel guilty from—how far away was Sweden? Several hundred miles at least! But she smiled to herself at that thought; he had won in the end.

And now Santas were dying suspiciously – it felt like something was coming to a head, somehow. But right now all she was heading for was the night bus back to her lonely, tiny flat in Greenwich, from wherever Derek deigned to drop her off. Gone were the days of transport to your door after gigs – Derek had seen to that after the coup. He gave good reasons for it of course; but Alan and Darren had managed to do it previously. Perhaps his heart could be softened by the potential danger posed by Santa killers on the loose? But she doubted it.

5

Terence stood in front of the flint-nodule covered house near the seafront in the old part of Deal, Kent. He could hear the sea cascading on the stony beach, just over the rooftops of the 18th-century cottages, probably originally built for fishermen. It was a dull winter day, not too cold, but with a hint of possible snow in the air. He had never been to Deal before, never had any reason to; it was not really on the way to anywhere. Dover was close, which he had been to, or rather through, but had never had any reason to go the seven or so miles to this old Cinque Port. It was fairly attractive, but not particularly touristy; the pier looked distinctly unglamorous. Brighton would have been the more obvious place for a couple of queer ex-actors to end up, if seaside was their desire.

It was exactly this couple, however, whose house he was now standing in front of, if his information was correct – and it unfailingly was. He was dressed as a FedEx delivery man, having hacked into the company's delivery schedule and pre-empted the genuine deliverer. Not difficult; they encouraged customers to track their parcels online, and a phone call to the nearest office by a confused old man who had forgotten his delivery number resulted in it quickly being given, and the rest was easy. It had meant an overnight dash from Prestatyn, scene of his last triumph, but had worked out very nicely with his own 'delivery' schedule. This would be his first double-header, killing two birds with one stone. The metaphor was chillingly accurate.

Terence walked up the shell-lined path to the front door of Cockle Cottage, wondering vaguely which came first, the name or the owners. As a completely asexual being he had no strong feelings either way about homosexuality, but it did irk him the way gay innuendo was seen as OK in the modern liberal world, but the same thing in a heterosexual context was old-school comedy, frowned upon and considered sexist. He was therefore no fan of Julian Clary, but found the *Carry On*s amusing in a sweet, old-fashioned sort of way. Which was a pity, because it was an ex-*Carry On* actor and his partner he was about to murder, rather than Julian Clary.

He took a deep breath, as any good actor would before stepping on to the stage, and rang the bell.

It was the ex-actor who answered the door, face lighting up when he saw the parcel. At least he was excited just before he died, Terence thought.

'Ooo, that was quick, you are efficient,' squealed the ageing thespian, 'I wasn't expecting you so soon. You're lucky to catch us, we were just about to take a stroll along the prom. We like our morning constitutionals, don't we Geoffrey?'

'Yes dear, whatever you say dear,' Geoffrey replied with mock resignation, raising his eyebrows at Terence conspiratorially. He seemed as camp and effete as his partner, and about the same age; there was obviously no butch/bitch dynamic in this relationship.

'Ooo, he's like an early Father Christmas, isn't he Geoffrey? Just a little on the thin side. You ought to build yourself up me lad! Lugging those heavy parcels about will get you all butch and muscley. Eventually. Now what have you got for us in your sack, Santa?'

The unprompted mention of 'Santa' and 'sack' took Terence aback; it was as if they knew what he was planning to do. 'Uh…I don't know,' he forced out, staring dumbly at the two elderly men, an actor who had suddenly forgotten his lines, thrown off course by the wrong cue.

'Well open it up and show us then, you 'nana!' Geoffrey teased. 'Or haven't you got the strength?'

Terence came back to the task in hand; the relief of lines remembered, back on track again.

'Oh, by the way gents, talking of Santa, is it true you both were Santas in Lapland at one point?'

The two ageing board-treaders collapsed into fits of giggles at this. 'Ooo you are awful – but we like you!' the ex-*Carry On*er tittered. 'How did you know that? We thought we had kept that secret! Yes, you're right duckie; we both did a season up there, among the Northern Lights and the huskies – and that was just the men! Yes, ten years ago it was, finances were getting a bit stretched, if you know what I mean. Way too cold for me, I have to say. You enjoyed it though, didn't you Geoffrey? You liked being wrapped up in your winter woollies!'

Geoffrey offered the by now usual response.

This friendly banter did have an effect on Terence; he wanted to shut them up. He was not sure if it made him hate them more, or made him want to get on with it in case his resolve weakened; either way, his next move stopped the banter in its verbal tracks. Reaching into his brown uniform jacket, he quickly pulled out a fearsome looking Beretta 92FS pistol, and pointed it menacingly at the two men. 'Shut up. Stand in the middle of the room, back to back.' He spoke in a quiet voice, but dripping with venom.

'Ooo, what do you mean? What are you playing at luvvie? Is that…?'

'I said shut up!' Terence now yelled. 'Fucking shut up! Now do as I say, stand over there, back to back, or I will use this fucking thing!'

His tone left no room for discussion; the two men did what they were told, terrified, wondering what the hell this young psychopath was going to do. They had been burgled a few times before, but had never seen the perpetrator, and had certainly never been threatened with a gun before. If they had had any inkling of his plans they would certainly have offered some resistance, and certainly not kept quiet.

The young psychopath now ripped open the box he had been delivering, keeping his revolver trained on the two trembling men, and pulled out a big roll of very strong duct tape. He then taped the men's hands together, then their bodies, starting at the ankles, as they stood obediently back to back. Given that he had to use both hands for this process, there were opportunities for braver men than these two to have made an attempt to escape, or try and disarm him; but these elderly actors were too old, terrified or unused to physical conflict to offer any resistance. Their hope was that co-operation would be their salvation, and that Terence would leave them tied up when he left the house with as many of their valuables as he could carry in his sack, which he now pulled out of the box. He laid it on the floor beside the two men, trussed up like Siamese mummies.

'Stand on this!' he commanded, motioning with the pistol.

'W-what are you going to do? You can have whatever...'

'I said shut the fuck up,' Terence repeated, this time through gritted teeth, 'and stand on this bloody sack.' The adjective was almost appropriate. The two men shuffled over as best they could, till they were standing on the bottom of the opened sack, which looked like old-fashioned hessian but on closer inspection was actually some sort of polythene, made to look like the traditional brown bag. Both still hoped they would survive the encounter, that the psycho would clean them out, and they would be discovered at some later point, shaken but basically OK.

His next action threw doubt on that hypothesis. Terence stuck a big bit of duct tape over the mouth of each ex-Santa, then pulled the sack up and over them, sealing it at the top with as much tape as he felt rendered it airtight. The two were now standing, completely trussed up, breathing severely restricted by the tape over their mouths, slowly suffocating in a completely airtight black hell, unable to do anything but possibly jump around, if they could work out how to do that in unison, without words. Or possibly fall over and roll around. It would certainly test how compatible with each other they were, Terence thought, and how good their improvisational skills were. Somehow they did not strike him as the kind of actors who had spent years at an expensive drama school doing all sorts of pointless trust games; these two could probably not improvise their way out of a paper bag, let alone a mock-hessian sack.

Terence guffawed at that thought. He did not really care if the men died or not; he thought they probably would, both using up what little air there was in the sack, unable to call for help. The best they could hope for was eventually being heard bumping against the walls or door. But the room he had chosen was not adjacent to another house or the street, and he already knew the two elderly gents did not have many visitors. The real FedEx man was a possibility, but chances were he would just leave a note saying he had called and the occupants were out. That seemed to be company policy in every case anyway.

'Happy Christmas!' Terence shouted as he closed the front door behind him, making sure the lock was on, and nothing looked untoward about the house. It was all going swimmingly, maybe too easily; he had heard and seen the news reports on his activities, but no one had a clue who he was, or what he was doing, even less why. There was always a chance he would be caught, he supposed, but that would more likely be by luck than judgement. His opinion on the intelligence and efficiency of the law enforcement agencies was not high. And by then he would probably have done most of what he wanted to do anyway. He threw the realistic replica pistol into a building skip he passed; it would be covered by broken bricks and concrete before anyone started looking for it, if they ever did. He caught himself whistling as he walked down the street towards where he had parked his dad's old Sierra, still registered in his father's name; he never whistled! Did not even think he could! What tune was it? He searched his limited musical memory banks. Yes: 'Santa Claus is Coming to Town'. He is; oh yes he is.

6

Phaedra jostled her way through the crowds of foreigners and shoppers that thronged the West End of London, en route to the Landmark Hotel, and the next murder mystery. Did she imagine it, or were the crowds thinner than usual for this time of year; and were the natives in even shorter supply? It was a Friday, 12 December, and the streets and shops of London should have been rammed. Not that they weren't – stupid people still got stupidly in her way – but there did not seem to be the same pre-Christmas buzz as usual. She could not stand people who loitered in London, getting in the way of busy people like her. Everyone should be made to walk quickly in the metropolis, it was a place of urgency and work, not dawdling; or perhaps the pavements could be segregated according to walking speed? She had done this in a PR stunt for Jameson's Whiskey once, the idea meant to be seen as silly; Phaedra thought it was eminently practical.

She had done a lot of that kind of silly PR work over the years, guerrilla advertising it could be called; ostensibly doing something, like a protest or a club or a society, whilst obliquely advertising something else. The knack of slipping the name of the true advertiser into any TV, radio or newspaper interview she did as the protester et cetera, was a large part of the skill. The rest of it did not need to be particularly believable: the media was always looking for quirky stories to fill its pages/airtime, and did not look too closely into any story if it seemed publishable. She had been a Professor of Youthspeak, of Adult Play Psychiatry, a personal reader, a water hose diviner, a protester on behalf of garden gnomes at the Chelsea Flower Show, a member of the Dennis the Menace Fan Club, and many, many more; all with the hope of surreptitiously getting publicity for the real client. She had been very good at it, happy to talk bollocks to the public and the media whilst keeping a straight face. And the money was good, till worldwide recession meant that companies put their dwindling resources into more demonstrably quantifiable advertising. Pity; she had enjoyed making a living by lying to the Great British Public.

The *Evening Standard* headlines shrieked 'Carry On Star Murdered!' from every newsstand; Phaedra had already heard the story on the radio that morning, and wondered if – no, was certain that – it was linked to the other Santa murders. Somehow it had to be. Pity; he was her second-favourite *Carry On* actor, after Kenneth Williams. The other murdered man hardly got a mention, of course. She would be surprised if he had ever worked as a Santa, certainly not since his *Carry On* days; but you never knew. He was the complete opposite of the jolly, rotund present-giver, in every possible way! Unless the murders – and she was pretty sure they were murders, coincidence could not possibly stretch that far – were not actually connected by Santa, but something else? Someone was just anti-thespian? She had a certain amount of sympathy with that position herself. Or anti-gay? She was not certain all the dead actors were of that persuasion, but being actors it was a definite possibility.

It was a half-hour walk between Charing Cross station and the hotel, Phaedra walking because she had the time, it saved money, and the tube would have been horribly busy at that time. If she had not walked, she might not have seen the new headline on the newsstands for the later editions of the *Standard*: 'Panto Star Dies on West End Stage!' A quick peruse of the front page told her: yes, he was famous, he was a large, older man, playing the principal comic role in the show, and he had dropped dead on the stage, in the matinee performance of *Dick Whittington (And His Cat)*, at one of the few pantos showing in the West End that Christmas, in the middle of the allegedly comic 'You Can Ring My Bell' song. Apparently the rest of the cast assumed he was drunk, as usual; as they were mostly lower-grade soap stars, and were doing this solely for the money, this was not considered unprofessional. A calling card with '#7' was later discovered in the lining of his wig. Gulp. She was not sure which of her murder theories that backed up, but it certainly made the whole business more grotesque.

She walked into the foyer of the suitably impressive Landmark bang on 6.00, as instructed, to see Derek apparently arguing with a member of staff, who looked like some sort of manager. He even seemed to be raising his voice. This was most unlike her erstwhile team leader; he was normally servile and respectful to hotel staff, getting his way by flattery and obsequiousness rather than force. Phaedra virtually sidled up to the gesticulating, fast-reddening, would-be modern day actor-manager, and noticed Peg and Malcolm, the rest of tonight's cast, had also equally sidled to a safe distance from their chief, trying to look nonchalant (and elsewhere) in their embarrassment. She gave them a quizzical look as she completed her sidling. The minor manager, if indeed he was, remained pretty calm in the face of Derek's blustering.

'But we have been booked to do it! We only have the props and actors for this plot, we can't do another at such short notice. It's only a game at the end of the day, it doesn't mean anything!'

The minor manager, who was also much shorter and younger than the angry thespian, allowed Derek to finish his rant, then calmly said, as if he had already said it several times, 'The hotel management cannot allow your company to perform *Who Killed Father Christmas?* in the current climate of opinion.'

'But – but it's only a name, you silly man. We don't really kill anyone! It's just a bloody game! Everyone knows no one really gets murdered. And this is our *profession*!'

'Don't you think it might be a *little* tasteless to perform *this* particular "plot" at this time?' the M.M. intoned, with barely detectable undertones of sarcasm.

'Oh God, it's only entertainment. Just a game at the end of the day. And at least in ours the villain is unmasked in the end!' the blustering apologist expostulated, unaware of the ludicrousness of his excuse.

'Really sir? Well perhaps your *talents w*ould be better employed at

Scotland Yard. I am sure they would welcome your obviously remarkable insights into this particularly baffling case.' *Superb*, thought Phaedra; *sign him up!*

'Look mate, don't get sarcy with me,' Derek rasped, resorting to the proletarian as the layers of servility quickly slipped away. 'I demand to see the manager!' Ah, the riposte of scoundrels.

'I *am* the manager, sir,' the diminutive functionary replied, in tones of resignation; he had obviously had to do that line before.

'Well…there must be someone above you,' Derek blustered, making the metaphorical physical by looking over the shorter man's head. 'I demand to see the over-manager!'

'The *Over-Manager* sir?' said in the tones in which one addresses a particularly stupid child. 'Well, it just so happens that the CEO of Landmark Hotels (Worldwide) Plc is visiting us at the moment. And she is currently standing just over there. I am sure she would be interested in your predicament.' Both men turned to where he indicated, to see a tall woman of a certain age, so sharply dressed her creases could slice cucumbers, power exuding from every centimetre of her shoulder pads, marching purposefully towards them. Derek visibly braced himself; this was not the sort of 'Over-Manager' he had envisaged.

'Is there a *problem*, Cedric?' the creature purred, the word pronounced as one would describe dog excreta on one's shoe. And in an American accent. This threw Derek even more, and his jaw sagged open foolishly. Oh how Phaedra was enjoying this.

'Ah, Ms Mansberger. Very sorry to bother you. Mr…?' ('Severn', sheepishly) 'here and his travelling players' (even Phaedra baulked at that description) 'wish to perform an…entertainment?...here this evening, entitled *Who Killed Father Christmas?* I believe.'

'Pardon me?'

'They want to perform an entertainment—'

'Called?'

'*Who Killed Father Christmas.*' 'I thought you said that.'

The six foot (in huge heels and shoulder pads – a sideline as a dominatrix a distinct option, thought Phaedra) American Amazon now turned her steely eyes on a visibly shrinking Derek.

'Mr – Seven?' she enquired in soft, questioning tones.

'Yes, that's right, it's a murder mystery event, for Chase Manhattan' (no flicker of respect in Ms Mansberger's green eyes at the name drop) 'we are due to start at…'

'A *what* event?' Brevity was becoming Ms M's trademark.

'Murder mystery – you know, someone gets murdered, well, actually, several people get murdered, and everyone has to try to…'

'Do we pay you for this?' Eyes narrowing to green slits – snakelike, Phaedra thought.

'Well no, not directly, Chase Manhattan…'

'Good. I am pleased we are not paying for this kind of crap, Cedric.' (Visible relief from the diminutive sub-manager.) 'Mr Sevenn,' she now said quietly, pointedly and menacingly, holding Derek's cowering eyes with her own, 'you may not be aware, but several men, many of them actors, have been murdered recently in this country, and the common theme seems to be Santa Claus, or as you say, Father Christmas. What you propose to do this evening is possibly the sickest thing I have ever heard of. I think you even outdo admirers of Charles Manson. I will not have *any* of my hotels associated with you or your bunch of sicko failed actors' (*Steady on!* thought Phaedra, *No need to push the truth so far, girlfriend!*) 'ever again. Now get the hell out of here, and take your shit props and sidekicks with you.'*Couldn't have put it better myself*, thought Phaedra.

She could see the dilemma on Derek's features – try and save face in front of the rest of the actors, who he hoped regarded him as some kind of leader, and risk being humiliated even more by this devil woman and her grinning sidekicks; or just accept defeat and retreat with tail between legs, a sort of damage limitation exercise. He looked for support from his team, but found what looked suspiciously like amusement on their faces; then back at the Mighty Mansberger, whose eyes were still fixed on his quivering face. He opened his mouth to say – what? We will never know; because the CEO snapped, 'Just get out of here. Cedric, get security.' Security seemed more than happy to manhandle the protesting thespian into the street – probably less trouble than a fat drunk businessman – and Phaedra, Peg and Malcolm offered no resistance, but followed meekly behind the cacophony.

Whilst not exactly throwing Derek on to the gleaming wet pavement, he was ejected out the front door with enough alacrity to startle a few passers-by. Quite literally dusting himself down, Derek seemed to expect vocal support from his team members – but got silent nonplussedness instead. Malcolm picked up scattered folders and papers and handed them back to his 'boss', barely concealing a smirk as he did so. 'She was a bit rough, I suppose,' was the best he could come up with, 'but she's got a point...I suppose?'Derek was completely lost for words. He had hoped for some support from 'his' actors, and got absolutely nil. The betrayal stunned him; after all he had done for this bunch of never-beens, getting all this work and employing them out of a vague sense of loyalty towards them, when he could have been selfishly advancing his career on the London stage – or even in films! He had recently got an agent, who had got him a part in a student film – but a good part, at the Bournemouth Film School, one of the more prestigious in the country – and a meteoric rise to stardom was possibly just round the corner; but he had put his burgeoning career on hold so he could keep *Murder on the Menu* going, partly to give these no-hopers work! How could they be so ungrateful? Did they not realise just how much he was sacrificing, basically for them?

'Wow, she was the CEO? What a woman. I want to grow up to be her. In fact, I think I'll go back in and ask her on a date!' Phaedra revelled in Derek's discomfort, pushing all the buttons she could. References to lesbianism unsettled him, especially hers.

'Um – will we still get paid for this?' Peg enquired tentatively, vocalising what everyone else was thinking. 'Only I turned down work in my bar tonight, thinking I would get more for this. I mean I'm sorry for what happened and everything' (a vague gesture towards the pavement and Derek, linking the two) 'but we could've done another plot, I suppose. It was a bit tasteless really, wasn't it, the Father Christmas plot?'

The others nodded and grunted in agreement, watching the now bedraggled figure of their erstwhile leader for some sort of reaction. Derek was a man for whom feelings and emotions had been continually repressed, probably since day one; the archetypal middle-class Englishman he professed to despise. Now was the closest anyone had ever seen to him actually exploding, and the fact he was obviously struggling with his inner volcano made it all the more smirkable. Despite the darkness his face was visibly purple, his team's betrayal stoking the fires of eruption even more. There was a sort of callous fascination as everyone watched to see if this would finally be his Krakatoa moment. His face twitched, his hands clenched and unclenched. For what seemed like – well, quite a long time – everyone was held in a sort of spell by the tension, till Phaedra could stand it no longer, and blurted out, 'Well I'm off to a new S&M club then, just opened in Soho. It's called "Humiliation". Anyone fancy coming?' Then she ran off down the street, Derek's roars receding in her ears. The volcano had finally erupted, S&M references piercing the final piece of Derek's crust. *Probably do him good*, she thought as she skipped along the wet London pavement, towards a non-existent club.

7

Saturday, 13 December, should have been the busiest shopping day of the year. For Terence it was certainly *one* of the busiest, but shopping was not the appropriate verb, although he did cross a few items off his list. It started in Newcastle first thing in the morning, in Fenwick's, for a long time the Toon's most prestigious department store; the Harrods of Geordieland, if you like. Or don't. Terence hardly noticed the scarcity of shoppers as he walked briskly up Grainger Street, or the fact that most of the visible ones seemed to be hurrying even more than he was, and had a furtive, worried look about them. He knew exactly where he was going, and how to get there.

He timed his arrival at the staff entrance to coincide with a gaggle of chattering shop girls, who paid him not the slightest bit of attention as he walked through the blue door with them. Security had not yet been tightened sufficiently to prevent this, and his spotty geekitude ensured none of the girls gave him a second glance. Some not even a first; tales of drunken activities the previous night held their attention. This was Newcastle, after all. Terence quickly located the staff toilet, where he donned a ubiquitous blue overall over his clothes in a cubicle. He did not have the correct staff pass, but a slightly dirty overall gets you most places in the staff areas of most large shops, he had discovered. He then found his way to the underground loading bay, where he knew Ken Stott, the regular Fenwick's Santa, had special permission to park his antiquated Volkswagen Beetle for the duration of his stint. Ken was also a children's entertainer, and the Beetle was perceived as a comedy car, in his eyes at least. More Walt's 'Herbie' than Adolf's 'People's Car'.

Terence had brought an adjustable spanner with him, prepared to tinker with whatever machinery was down there if seen and challenged, but luckily the bay was empty, all the deliveries having been done in the early hours. So he waited in the shadows until, about 9.30, the yellow, slightly dilapidated Beetle, with 'The Great Pissarto' emblazoned on both sides – even the roof! – drove down the ramp into the darkened bay. *God, the man has no class*, thought the young assassin; *oh, how he deserves to die. Crimes against entertainment if nothing else.*

Ken – a large man, needing no padding for this particular role – was struggling to extricate himself from behind the wheel of the small car when a young, slightly spotty, but friendly and helpful young man in a blue overall appeared beside the open door. 'Hello, Mr Stott. I've been told to escort you up to the staff area today. A sort of security provision, like. What with all these murders going on.' Terence had even mastered the North-East accent; the Internet is a wonderful tool to a criminal. What an actor he could have been; in many ways, he was.

'Why that's right nice of you man,' replied the portly present purveyor, in similar tones. 'You couldn't take me sack and costume while you're at it, could you? Them stairs is canny steep.' His victims all played into his hands, thought Terence. He led the way across the murky underground bay to a nondescript, scruffy door, and opened it. 'That's not the staff entrance is it, bonny lad?' asked the spurious Santa. 'No, not the usual one Mr Stott. I've been asked to take you up the emergency exit so no one can see you. Just a security precaution, like.' Ken did not question this assertion, but followed meekly behind his executioner. *Veritable lambs to the slaughter*, thought the young psychopath. He led the wheezing leviathan up the steep stairs, keeping just ahead of Ken, till he was almost at the top – then suddenly turned around and kicked him in his red, breathless face with as much force as he could muster.

For a split-second (if that means an exceedingly short space of time), Terence caught sight of the look of bewildered surprise on Ken's visage – then he was hurtling head-over-heels back down the stairs he had recently ascended so laboriously. But much, much quicker. Being steep, there was no chance of Ken stopping before he reached the bottom; the only snag to Terence's plan would be if the Rotund Red One somehow became wedged in the narrow stairwell. But all went to plan, and Ken ended up in a heap, blocking the doorway. A cursory investigation revealed he was still breathing, if erratically and shallowly, as blood oozed from several facial wounds; a couple of limbs seemed to be bent at unusual angles. But our Ter was prepared for this; slipping a latex glove on to his right hand, he withdrew his rather large adjustable spanner from its designated pocket, and fetched Ken a terrific blow to the temple. The crack of bone splitting was audible; Terence hoped not too much so. More blood gushed, from the new wound, creating a bit of a puddle on the bottom step. Terence once more investigated the breathing process; finding none this time, he pocketed the spanner, reached into Ken's sack, found his white beard (in fairly scruffy condition, Terence noticed, critically) and stuffed it into the ex-Santa's mouth. He then stepped over the inert body, opened the door, and emerged once again into the darkened loading bay. First one off his list.

But for the first time on his Christmas spree, things did not go perfectly for the psychopathic genius. Ken's stairway tumble must have been louder than Terence had bargained for, because a pimply young trainee emerged from the staff entrance just as Terence was disappearing back out into the sunlight. He spotted the back of the fast-retreating 'janitor', who removed his overalls as he hurried, noticing the speed of his exit. Slightly puzzled by that behaviour, whilst looking at the emergency exit door, he was equally surprised to see a pool of red liquid emerging from under it. The lad wrenched the door open – then turned and vomited at the sight that met his eyes.

Meanwhile, the hero of our tale was making his way along the A69 to the other side of the country – Carlisle, to be precise. Arriving about 10.30, he made his way quickly to The Lanes, the city's biggest shopping mall. How Terence hated that word, and its American-ness. He hated all the lazy Americanisms marching into modern British culture, to be honest. A man of catholic hates, one might say. He had changed into his ubiquitous anyshop uniform, and sat outside one of the many eateries scattered around the central part of the edifice, sipping a latte. One of the few luxuries he allowed himself. This place actually had a grotto, which the conservative side of Terence's character approved of; but in this case Santa protection rather than child protection should have been the issue at stake. A grotto meant Elves, or other such Christmas helpers. And this would be Terence's route to the Great Man, rather than an added layer of protection for the Bearded One.

He knew, from hours of dedicated Internet research, that Jenny Telfer, 19-year-old student with a slightly embarrassing Christmas job, started her Elf stint at 11.00 today. And he knew what she looked like, even comatose; thank you, Facebook! At 10-to-11 she appeared, slightly dishevelled and flustered, pushing her way through the pushchairs ('buggies' to the younger) towards said grotto.

Just as she was about to enter the 'staff entrance' to the grotto, ready to reappear as a mythical green creature minutes later, Terence tapped her on the shoulder. Turning quickly, ready to rebuff some stupid enquiry from an equally stupid parent or child, she was somewhat startled to see a slightly geeky-looking youth, of similar age to herself, poking a plate of fairy cakes tentatively into her face.

'Oh – these are for, y'know, *Santa*,' the youth stammered uncertainly, 'from Millie's Cookies, ower there,' (pointing vaguely behind him; there was bound to be a Millie's Cookies somewhere in the complex). 'We heard he had a sweet tooth, and thought he might like these, specially with all this horrible stuff going on wi' Santas.' The plate hovered uncertainly inches from Jenny's nose; there was a nice smell of baking, and was that marzipan?

'Why that's right nice of you, ta,' answered the slightly blushing student, 'I'm sure *Santa* will appreciate *getting* a present for a change!'

'Oh yeah, great; they're not very big, tell him they're best eaten in one mouthful.'

'Alright, I will. I might be round the shop for some myself later, if they're as good as they smell!' Was she almost flirting? A novel experience for Terence.

'Oh aye – of course – come round any time you like, I'm on all day,' he blushingly replied.

'Alright then. See you later. And…have a nice day.' And with that Jenny disappeared into the secret world of the grotto.

Oh how wonderfully ironic, thought the young monster: *Santa's demise brought to him by one of his own Elves!* Terence hoped Jenny would not have one of the cakes herself – at least not until after she had seen the effect it had on her Master – she seemed quite nice really, and had even been polite to him. An unusual experience in his troubled life. But if she did – well, it was collateral damage, couldn't be helped; and she was a Santa-ist lackey, after all, so probably deserved it. In every war there are innocent casualties.

Terence had a bit of spare time in his busy shopping spree, and could not resist the temptation to watch the results of his generosity; so he returned to his half-drunk latte, hoping no one had taken much notice of his elfin interaction. He was breaking his own rules, but felt he could – no, should – cut himself a little slack, and have a bit of fun. Was success breeding carelessness? Anyway, he moved towards the back of the cafe, where he could not be spotted immediately, but could see pretty much everything that happened on the concourse.

And it happened quickly – the Fat Man must have bolted those poisoned cakes pretty promptly. Terence had just got down to the milky froth at the bottom of his cup when a distraught Jenny, in full Elf garb (she suited green, thought Ter) burst out of the front entrance of the grotto, startling a few children and adults waiting for an audience with the Kindest Man. 'Help! Get an ambulance! Santa's really ill! Is there anyone who can do first aid?' she blurted out breathlessly, to bemused nonchalance from kids and parents alike. Human reaction time can be fairly slow, especially for the unexpected occurrence. And, despite all recent events, this was unexpected in a Carlisle grotto.

So Jenny turned it up a notch 'SOMEONE GET A FUCKING AMBULANCE! SANTA IS DYING!' she roared. Terence was impressed by her vocal range; pity she would blame herself forever for the death of this particular Mr Christmas.

The Great British Public belatedly began to react, so Terence took the opportunity to sidle in the other direction. But he couldn't resist a final, self-satisfied glance back at the carnage he had caused – and in that brief glance his eyes locked with the stricken Jenny's. A sudden stab of realisation consumed her distraught face; and then he was gone. But maybe half a second too late.

Meanwhile, exactly 99 miles by the most direct route south, portly middle-aged Bob Lord was getting ready for his stint at the Blackpool

Rialto afternoon bingo session. He had been doing it for 20-odd years now; not the most glamorous job he had ever done, Bob reflected, but a job is a job, and when you get to my age you are thankful for anything you can get. And with a bad back and dodgy knees, Bob was grateful he was not struggling away at some manual job. His background as a stand-up comedian in the northern clubs, when they had still existed, certainly helped his bingo calling; those middle-aged ladies loved an innuendo. And the old ones even more so! Though they often didn't get the wittier ones. There were even a few younger, quite fit women coming along nowadays, and Bob's flirtatious comments even struck a resonant chord there sometimes. And with the added seasonal reverie involved at this time of year – well, you never knew your luck.

The session started at 2.00, but Bob liked to get in early, sort out all the equipment, make sure the PA, et cetera was working properly; he was an old pro, after all. And the Rialto was one of the more prestigious bingo clubs in Britain's half-hearted response to Las Vegas: at least he didn't have to bring his own gear. Now that he seldom ventured on to the stand-up circuit, apart from the occasional charity gig, to people who had never heard of him, Bob was content to be a caller – it was still a chance to be in the limelight and be loved, after all, even though most of his admirers were a similar age to his mother. And sometimes not even as well preserved. Bob still had ambitions however, but now they only reached as far as the Tower bingo sessions – the apogee of Blackpool Bingo. Which possibly also meant the apogee of British Bingo. The Sunday night sessions were huge there, hundreds and hundreds of punters, even some men. The place itself was glitzy and glammy, some sessions linked up with the top clubs all over the country, so your audience could be in the thousands – as could the prize money, and the fee, for the right caller. The present incumbents were the aristocracy of the Bingo world, and Bob aimed to one day join their ranks. So he knew he always had to be on the ball, so to speak, and perform well, no matter how lowly the club was – reputations are hard won, but can be easily lost. Thus Bob always wanted to be seen as supremely Professional, even to the extent of keeping up his Equity membership.

Which is why he was not surprised when a young, skinny, besuited man approached him in the backstage corridor at about half past one, as he was carrying the numbered balls towards the stage. He claimed to be from the British Gambling Commission, doing a spot check on the premises, to ensure fairness, and that no jiggery-pokery was going on. Though he did not use that term. Very professional, thought Bob; usually these things are announced in advance, but surprise spot checks would be more effective. Bob therefore approved, and did as he was told. Professional and co-operative at all times.

'Mr Lord, isn't it?' the official stated, matter-of-factly.

'Oh yes, that's me,' the ex-comedian replied, glad to have been recognised, if only by a Government Inspector. 'Chief caller here at the Rialto, as I'm sure you know. Can I help you at all?'

Terence hated the current trend of sticking an 'at all?' on the end of every request, especially by shop staff, but metaphorically bit his tongue and carried on, in a quietly assertive manner.

'Just doing a spot check on the balls, Mr Lord. I'm afraid there was a complaint by a member of the public last week, and it is our statutory duty to look into these things, as I am sure you understand. We wouldn't want the Rialto to lose its bingo licence, would we?'

'N-no, of course not.' Inwardly Bob shrank; losing licence = losing job, and chance of the Tower gone forever. 'W-was it at one of my sessions at all?'

More inward grimacing by the Inspector. 'To be honest I am not sure, Bob. It was more of a general complaint. But we have to look into everything. Could you just hold the bowl while I have a quick rummage about?'

'O-of course, be my guest'. Bob's relief at the last comment was enormous; the Tower still beckoned. And his gratefulness to this young official blinded poor old Bob's mind to the lack of any official ID shown by the questioner. At that moment he would have done anything to please the Inspector and keep the licence, and the Inspector knew it. He was a very shrewd judge of human character, like all top actors.

Bob did not want to be seen to be watching the Inspector's actions too carefully; it might seem like nervousness, some sort of admission of guilt. So he held the big Perspex bowl with both hands in front of him, looking over Terence's head as he 'rummaged'. Therefore he did not see exactly what happened next.

'Oh – what's this?' the Inspector questioningly said, holding up two red and white balls. Both with the number '25' on them. He looked askance at Bob.

Bob's face assumed the colour of driven snow. Or lack of it. 'I-I-I've no idea!' he managed to splutter, eyes transfixed by the two apparently identical balls.

'Oh, that's not very good is it?' Terence stated with raised eyebrows, looking directly into the confused caller's face. 'I wonder if there might be any more? Um – I'm not allowed to put my hands in my pockets while I'm doing this, in case of any impropriety, you know, so could you – um – just hold this in your mouth for a minute?' The eyebrows remained up, questioning, but demanding the answer 'yes'.

Which is what Bob said; co-operation and professionalism at all times, especially in this dicey situation. If there were two balls with the same number, as it seemed there were, that was not his fault; though the Inspector would not know that. So, obligingly and co-operatively, Bob opened his moustachioed mouth, and Terence 'popped' the offending ball in. How he hated the ubiquity of that word; worse than 'at all?' But in this case it was the most apposite, as he continued to rummage.

Bob was now looking intently at the Inspector's hands, no pretence of disinterest; but of course he could not see beyond the cuffs, as the hands were submerged in the sea of numbered balls. Therefore the exact mechanics of how Terence now produced two balls numbered '12' was invisible to him.

'Oh. Dear. There's more. Number 25, and now 12. Christmas Day!' The official spoke almost jovially.

'You were a Santa for a while, weren't you Bob?'

With his mouth full of ball, all the embarrassed caller could say was 'Ah!', and nod his head.

'Thought so. Well, same thing applies, I'm afraid. Could you put this in your mouth too? Sorry, but it shouldn't be for long'.

Bob's eyebrows narrowed in concern, but given the situation he felt he had to concur, so the second ball was 'popped', and the procedure continued. Bob was now feeling fairly silly, as well as very worried; but his Professionalism and respect for authority prevented him from doing anything but carry on holding the bowl while the Inspector rummaged. He had been in several silly situations before, and this would just be another; make a funny anecdote when it was all over. If it turned out all right, of course.

Which now seemed less probable, as Terence produced two blue and white balls, both with the number '20' on them.

'This is not looking good, Bob,' he stated the obvious. 'Room for any more in there?' he asked/commanded, with a lightness of tone which did not match Bob's mood; and without waiting for reply he pushed the third ball into the already full mouth. Bob was now getting very concerned, about his breathing as much as the Rialto's licence; this was going too far, surely?

'Just hold them there a minute Bob, this will all be over soon,' stated the suited 'Spector. Bob kept holding the bowl; dropping the balls was the biggest debacle in the Bingo business, and he was, if nothing else, Professional.

'Bingo!' Terence suddenly expostulated, pulling out two more red and white balls, with the same number on. 'Four! Twenty, then four! Twenty-oh-four! That's when you were in Lapland, wasn't it, Bob? Fulfilling all those children's dreams? Proving that Santa really did exist? Well, I'm afraid he doesn't any more.' And with that he rushed at the totally confused caller, grabbed his hair with his left hand, and forced the fourth ball into the already over-extended mouth with his right.

Bob could hold the bowl no longer; it hit the floor with a boing, bouncing, coloured balls scattering everywhere. Then so did he, slipping on a few of the balls and hitting the floor heavily, being a big man. Terence was on him in a flash, tearing off a strip from his faithful duct tape reel, covering Bob's hirsute mouth, already bursting with four balls inside. Bob clawed at Terence's hands, but he was already in the process of suffocating, being unable to spit out the balls. The 'Inspector' now put his foot on the prone caller's throat, which the quickly weakening Bob was unable to move. He squirmed around for a while, face quickly turning purple, like a harpooned whale thrashing about in its death throes; then he squirmed no more, and his arms fell by his sides, lifeless. Terence removed his foot from Bob's throat, shook out the spare balls from his suit sleeves, dusted the jacket down, stepped over the prone body, and walked briskly down the corridor. Those early years in his bedroom with his Paul Daniels magic set were paying off in ways he never could have imagined as a friendless child.

Three down by lunchtime; on schedule. If only life was as efficient as me, he sighed.

8

At almost exactly the same time, given the one-hour difference, Barry was sitting on a high stool at the bar of the Brunkullans Krog Med bar in Ostersund, the nearest town of any size to Ytterhogdal. He was drinking a 'Fallen Angel' beer, a premium ale from the (fairly) local Jamtlands Bryggeri brewery. He had always been an ale man, a rock amongst a turbulent sea of lager these days. It was unusual for him to be in town this early on a Saturday, and even more unusual to be in a bar this early. He had the place to himself, the barman exchanging a few pleasantries when he first arrived (in English! How do they always know?), then leaving him alone as he struggled through the foreign news section of *Svenska Dagbladet*, one of the country's quality dailies.

It was of course sub-zero outside, which partly explains why Barry was sitting in a warm bar; but it could equally have been a cafe, his love of coffee having increased during his Scandinavian sojourn. But for some reason he wanted a bar that day; he had decided to put his shopping off till later. Beer is of course fairly expensive in all the ex-Viking kingdoms, but Barry was being paid Swedish wages, so it pretty much equalled itself out. Beer was pretty expensive in British pubs too. But he was still nursing rather than quaffing it.

Ever since the news of the Santa 'murders' came through on Wednesday, Barry had been forced to think of the events of this time 10 years ago, whether he wanted to or not. Sven constantly mentioned it at work, and the TV news was full of it. They loved 'quirky' British news stories. Barry did not watch much TV, preferring to read or listen to music; but he could not help catching snatches of the story, like you always manage to accidentally hear the score correctly when your football team has lost a vital game. He was not really concentrating now, as the paper tried to find a new angle on the eternal tragedy of the Middle East.

Ten years ago! Unbelievable. How time had flown. With nothing much to show for it, apart from a healthy bank balance. Which was at least something; it had been a rare occurrence in his performing days. But mentally, spiritually, personally, was he any further forward? At least he was not thinking about P. for 90% of his waking hours, which had been the case in the worst years, shortly after they officially split up. It had not quite been a nervous breakdown, but fairly close, he supposed. He had never really understood what the term meant before; he thought he did now. Mulling everything over, wondering what he should have said, what she had meant by that, what might have happened if he had done or said that, what could still happen, how she could think or say that, wishing he had not done or said that – oh God it had been awful, and nothing could break the cycle of thought; not even football. Friends all told him to give it up and move on, but that was easier said than done. He was flogging a dead horse, and knew it, but continued to flog, every now and again encouraged by something she might say or do. He did not suppose she was doing it deliberately, but she played it perfectly: he was like putty in her hands. When his friend Vera told him that he was in danger of becoming the sad clown who carries on loving someone who is mercilessly cruel to him, and all his friends know, and eventually despise his patheticness – that was a moment of clarity, when he realised he had to do something.

And now…was this another moment of clarity coming on, as he started his second Fallen Angel? The first one (moment of clarity that is, not beer) had seen him up sticks and come over to ABBA country, telling hardly anyone; he loved a theatrical exit. Or entry. Anything theatrical, to be honest. Apart from his fellow thespians, that is. Now… thinking of his time in Lapland as Santa 10 years ago, the arrangement for Phaedra to meet him on the frozen lake at Kemijarvi on Christmas Eve, her non-appearance, the return to Gatwick, the anger, the sadness, the crying, the forgiveness – oh, God, how bloody awful it had been! How had he become so besotted? She was not that beautiful really, and a funny shape all told, bit on the fleshy side; but at times she just oozed sex, even though she often just seemed to want to cuddle. Oh, the nights of frustration, punctuated by the occasional fantastic shag – well, he thought so anyway – which made him think she had changed her mind; but all the time she claimed she was in love with someone else – an alcoholic, gay, suicidal graffiti artist! How could he compete with that? And she also claimed she wanted to be a lesbian…how many bloody alarm bells should have been ringing? It should have been deafening, like being inside the Queen Elizabeth Tower when Big Ben (and all the other bells, let's not forget them) sound midnight. Or noon. But something had driven him on, relentlessly, towards mental destruction.

But now…five years later, events back in Britain forced those thoughts into Barry's head again. Had he really resolved it all, and regained his mental equilibrium, or just put it on hold while he immersed himself in his work and getting to know a foreign culture? Perhaps some kind of cleansing ceremony was needed, to wave it all goodbye once and for all? On the 10th anniversary of the pivotal event, perhaps? He smiled to himself; Phaedra would approve of a ceremony, particularly if it was a pagan one. He swigged down the rest of the Angel, left the paper, and walked out into the sub-arctic winter. Another theatrical event was on the cards.

Several hours later, and several hundred miles to the south-west, the object of Barry's ruminations was contemplating her costume for that evening's fancy dress party. Christmas themed, of course. The venue was also to the south-west of Phaedra's current position, but only a few miles away, in Richmond; but given the vagaries of trans-London transport, it would probably take as long to get there as flying to Sweden. And getting back afterwards…don't even go there, as the unoriginal say. Would it be worth the effort? she wondered; but she had to get out of her tiny bedsit on a Saturday night in the festive season, surely? The party was at the house of one of her lesbian feminist friends, with whom she had a lot of empathy; she just found them all a bit sincere and humourless. Phaedra could not help taking the piss and undercutting undue sincerity when confronted with it. She was not sure if it was one of her best or worst traits: depends on the viewpoint of the recipient, she supposed.

The title of the event was actually 'Mother Winterfest', to escape any paternalist or Christian references; Phaedra assumed a lot of green would be worn, spurning the supposed Coca-Cola-influenced red of the current male office holder. That at least made it slightly less controversial, given the current circumstances. A week ago she had envisaged sporting a red PVC outfit with a very short 'skirt' with white fur trim, and possibly fishnet tights and black thigh-length boots, to be both awkward and sexy, adjectives often applied to her, especially by Barry; but with the current carnage of the Red-Robed One even *she* recognised the bad taste involved in that interpretation. So it would have to be something else…something elfish, perhaps? She could still be green and sexy she supposed, though red was really the colour of lust. With perhaps a bit of black as well. The anarchist colours, of course! Maybe she could cobble something together from some of her old panto costumes, all of which she had kept.

These musings were interrupted by the strident ringtone of her phone: she had plumped for 'I Am What I Am', semi-ironically. Phaedra fished it out from under a pile of clothes (good thing it rang, she had no idea where she had put it), and looked at the screen. 'Murder on Menu'; unusual for Derek to phone on a Saturday, she usually got at least three days' notice of a booking. Unless someone had let them down at the last minute? Hopefully not another cancellation; bookings had thinned out noticeably since the recent events.

66

'Hello, Derek?' she said, in a questioning tone, not knowing what to expect.

'Ah – Phaedra – glad I got hold of you. You OK?' said the aspiring actor/entrepreneur, in a voice which sounded forcibly light to her ear.

'Ye-es', she replied somewhat guardedly. 'To what do I owe this pleasure? You haven't been jilted, have you? Professionally, I mean, of course.'

'Ha…ha! Funny you should say that! I mean not that I've been jilted – well, not literally of course! Ha-ha! No, Prudence is out tonight, as it happens, at some literary launch do I think. I'm not invited. She's— well…I'm just not invited.

'Um…about the other night…you know, at the gig at the Landmark… well, sorry I got so annoyed…' He coughed, waiting for a response from her, she supposed. She said nothing but 'Mmm', wondering where this was going.

'Well, I shouldn't have got so annoyed I suppose – very unprofessional – and I can see her point now – I was so immersed in the job I suppose, keeping the company going, show must go on, et cetera; ha! You know what I mean, you're an old pro.' (*Not as old as you*, thought P.).

'Well, um –' (deep inhalation) 'you know you said you were going to an…S&M club?'

'Ye-es; oh yes, of course! Called – now what was it called?' That thought at least was genuine; she could not remember the name of the imaginary club she had made up that night.

'Humiliation.' It had obviously lodged itself in Derek's head. 'How was it? Do you go often?' (At least he didn't say 'do you come often?')

'Mm…no, that was my first time actually.'

'Oh – but you've been to places like that before, haven't you? You're a woman of the world and all that kind of thing.' *Where is this leading?* Phaedra wondered; she had an inkling, but did not really believe it.

'Yes, I do indulge in a little fetishism and so forth now and again, Derek; you know how it is, one must explore every avenue, we only have a certain time here, la-la-la. Why? Do you want to come along some day?'

'Um – well – yes, why not? As you say, one must explore every avenue, would be rude not to, ha-ha!' (*Not as rude as actually going*, thought P.)

'Oh, *right*,' Phaedra extended the word as much as she could; she sensed a power transfer taking place, and was determined to enjoy it as much as she could. This had never happened before with Mr Murder on the Menu. 'Well, Derek, I would be happy to take you along next time I go. You've got to have the right gear for it though, they don't like tourists. You do understand that?'

'Ah, yes, well – *harrumph* – I uh – *cough* – have a few things already, from various plays I've been in, you know what I mean?'

'Oh really Derek? What plays were those then?'

'Oh well…um…em…I can't remember the names at the moment – it was a while ago…'

'Weeell…I must look at your CV sometime, I would love to know what they were. What gear have you got then?' How she was enjoying this.

'Well, I've got…em…a "gimp mask" I think they call it, some PVC pants, a dog collar, restraining belts with big shiny buckles, the odd whip or two, nipple clamps, an enema…that kind of thing.' Derek must have realised he was getting too carried away, because he stopped the list suddenly. Phaedra struggled to suppress a giggle; this was priceless.

'Must have been an interesting play, that one; and they let you keep the costume after? Very generous of them. And have you worn any of your "costume" recently? Does Pru like you to dress up in this kind of stuff?'

'Oh no, no, no,' Derek's reply was immediate and desperate. 'Oh no, she isn't into this sort of thing. No, not at all. In fact she – um – doesn't know I have this gear.'

'Where do you keep it then, Derek? Under the bed? In a secret trunk with a sign saying "Private! Keep Out! Derek's Secret Stuff!"?' Phaedra was playing Derek like a hooked salmon. Though, as a vegetarian, she did not like the simile.

'Well, let's just say I hope she never finds it. She kind of lives up to her name, if you know what I mean? I know you've never met her, but she's – well – mm – not particularly broad-minded, if you know what I mean.' It was certainly true that Phaedra had never met Derek's betrothed; a lot of the time she had doubts about her very existence, though some of the other murder actors claimed to have set eyes on the woman. Strong and forceful were the general adjectives used. Phaedra was beginning to see the truth of these reports; it seemed as if her erstwhile boss fell into the classic dom at work/sub at home category. But if Prudence was not going to play out that sexual fantasy for him, who did he expect to?

'So if we do go to a club Derek, you will have to play out the traditional slave/mistress syndrome, at least some of the time. Do you have someone in mind to play the mistress role? Or master?' Phaedra's mind was racing over the various possibilities; could Derek actually want a gay sub/dom fantasy? Her boss was becoming more interesting by the second.

'Well, I, eh, um, thought maybe *you* could?'

This was too much to bear. Phaedra collapsed on to the bed in a paroxysm of laughter, throwing the phone across the room in the process. She rolled about on her 'Elf' costume, tears of unrestrained mirth rolling down her slightly chubby face.

'Phaedra? Phaedra? You still there?' she could hear Derek squeaking out of the phone, now nestled in one of her large lacy bras on the carpet of her admittedly tiny bedroom. 'I can't hear you any more. You still there? Um – I can't hear you properly; if you can hear me…phone me back sometime. OK? Right, OK. Thanks! Bye.'

The phone went silent. Phaedra remained lying on the bed, staring at her somewhat tatty Christmas decorations, slowly calming down from her maelstrom of merriment, body still shaking slightly. This was an early Christmas gift; it was blackmail gold! Never more would Derek have any power over her; she could probably even choose her own fee for the jobs he would now *have* to give her. Her financial future was now assured, as long as *Murder on the Menu* carried on going, of course. David always assured them that the future was rosy, despite her fears that they had passed Peak Murder. Metaphorically, if not actually. Phaedra put the finishing touches to her Elf costume with renewed optimism. Santa had come early for her, and his present would last well beyond Christmas.

9

Eighteen hours later Phaedra was lying in the same position, but this time inside the double bed, which was only raised above floor-and-scattered-clothes-level by a wooden pallet. Some of the Sundays were scattered about the duvet; she allowed herself the luxury of a newspaper delivery on the Sabbath. It reminded her of home and her childhood, plus it gave a small income to an enterprising child. She had not remained in this position since The Phone Call, however; the Mother Winterfest party had been enlivened by her presence, she was more animated and jolly than usual, and had even snogged a tall Amazonian reindeer, and had her tits fondled. She loved that, to be honest; did not really matter who the fondler was. But not enough to return with the reindeer to her stable afterwards. She did get a certain amount of pleasure from tempting lesbians then turning them down; fanny-teasing she supposed it could be called. They probably hated her for it, and for claiming to be bisexual. But it unfortunately fitted into her usual behaviour patterns.

She had managed to return via a combination of night buses; a taxi would have been ludicrously expensive. Made the reindeer's proposition more attractive, but not quite enough. Falling into bed about 5.00, a bit pissed and wasted, she allowed herself a satisfied smirk about Derek before drifting off into oblivion. Now she was slowly coming round, cup of tea in hand, eyes beginning to focus on the words and pictures all around her. She liked a spread of journalistic opinion; today's contributions came from *The Observer*, *Mail on Sunday* and *Sunday Mirror*. No one could ever accuse her of being narrow-minded. The Santa Murders had now taken over completely; pages 1, 2, 3 and 4 at the very least were devoted to them in every rag, plus editorials and opinions, from virtually everyone who cared to voice one. More pictures in the tabloids of course; including ones of Colin and Harvey. Looked like their Spotlight actors' photos, she thought, therefore well out of date. But familiarity with those (albeit idealised) faces brought the whole carnage home to her. The *Carry On* actor of course featured prominently, his partner less so; every publication catalogued the variety of methods of murder with as much detail as they could muster. The whole thing was genuinely a Christmas gift to the press, both the sensational and the serious. The only difference was the adjectives used. Luckily there were no pictures of the actual bodies; but a few illustrations of sacks, beards, bells, et cetera were published, to remind their readers what those things were.

Opinion varied immensely, informed and uninformed; although as so little was known about the perpetrator(s), they were mostly completely uninformed. Never stopped people having opinions before, however, and did not now. The general theme of the *Mail*'s editorial was that they were the work of a rabid anti-consumerist fringe element; the sheer number of victims, and geographical spread, excluding the work of a single psychopath. Christmas is of course the height of consumerism, more so every year; Mr Claus, being the representative of that consumerism, which is destroying the planet and our souls, is therefore the main target. They even managed to dredge up some website which could be interpreted as vaguely supporting the killing spree, by a group calling itself 'Kill Christmas'. Apparently the police were currently investigating the members of said group, having nothing else to go on.

The *Mirror* went in another direction: it was all the work of anti-paedophile vigilantes, working in cahoots with each other. The paper rightly noted that all the victims had been playing the Red Gift-Giver for at least 10 years, beginning in an era where grottos were the norm, child safety was not such an issue, and kiddie-fiddling therefore more rife. Even sitting on Santa's knee was vaguely intimated to be pervy now. The campaigning red-top had looked into the pasts of several of the victims, sniffed around a bit, and found rumours of Inappropriate Behaviour in the cases of several; this was extrapolated to cover them all, just not having been revealed yet. Even the *Carry On* actor's name did not escape being tarnished in this way. The Nottingham Santa's discovery, with penis hanging out and pillow stuffed in mouth à la auto-erotic asphyxiation, served as the clincher. The perpetrators were probably survivors of sexual abuse, tired of not being believed, taking matters of revenge into their own hands.

The *Observer* took yet another line; could it be the work of extreme Christians, sick of the increasing materialism of the Lord's birthday, taking it further and further away from its original meaning? The 'Christ' in Christmas was almost completely eclipsed by the 'ta' in Santa, as presents were feverishly bought and grudgingly given at this time of year. In many children's minds Santa had become God-like, keeping watch over children, instantly knowing who had been Naughty or Nice, and dispensing giftly justice appropriately. Plenty of followers of Christ were on record saying how awful this was, and that we should get back to the former purity of the season of goodwill. Christmas lights and decorations all over the country bore no relation to the event being celebrated, but concentrated on presents being received – and I suppose given, but that did not seem to be the emphasis. And in the towns where the very name had been dropped in favour of something multi-faith: don't get them started. The paper had of course produced some prominent clergymen to say they doubted this, and that it was dreadful and non-Christian if it was in fact the case; a few extreme believers were also quoted saying that Mr Claus was the new Antichrist. Police claimed to be investigating these lines of enquiry as well.

Phaedra obviously did not know what to believe; none of the above theories completely held water to her mind. The sheer numbers were unbelievable: 12 in a week, as far as everyone knew. But there could be more waiting to be discovered. Bob the bingo caller did not appear to fit into any particular theory; but she would not be at all surprised if it turned out he had played the Round Red One at some point in his illustrious career. But why those particular incarnations of the Big Man, and not others? Was it a single, very mobile, killer, or several, just doing their bit in their local area?

Having tired of Christmas carnage, and having no interest in Sport, Fashion, Property or Travel (not the kind one finds in the supplements, anyway), our heroine made the momentous decision to stretch over and put the telly on. A small portable, very old-fashioned, but at least in colour. *The Andrew Marr Show* was on; it looked like it was about religion, as there appeared to be representatives of several denominations present. She identified some by their hats; she was a vicar's daughter, after all. Hat identification had been a somewhat esoteric part of her childhood lessons. But as she half-heartedly listened and watched, she realised that the Santa murders had hijacked even this august 'political' show. The Archbishop of Canterbury (a friend of her father) was saying that although he abhorred the recent events, in some way he could understand them! This of course brought instant condemnation from all the other religious representatives; the Greek Orthodox (big black hat, beard, beads) man being particularly censorious. Even the Archbish of York joined in the Bish-bashing; probably after his boss's job, thought P. Politics even at this time. The RC Archbish (little purple skull cap) tried to be placatory; but the Moderator of the General Assembly of the Church of Scotland (snappy title; made up for lack of distinctive headgear) was having none of that, and weighed into the head of the Church of England with evangelical zeal. *Poor old Cantab*, thought P.; that's what you get for trying to be all-embracing. If only the Rev. Ian Paisley had been there as well, we could have had a right royal ding-dong. The Muslim and Jewish representatives just sat back, shrugging their shoulders and smiling smugly. As for Hindus – maybe it was a monotheistic show only.

The contretemps was just beginning to die down, poor old Cantab mopping his brow with a hankie and trying vainly to loosen his dog collar, when the presenter, glad of the opportunity to regain control over the proceedings, interrupted his guests to introduce a live outside broadcast. It was from one of the 'leaders' of the Occupy movement, if it could be said to have such beings. Calling himself 'John Wilkes', probably not his real name, he stared reluctantly at the camera from underneath his grey hoodie hood. He read from a prepared statement, which appeared to be on a small packet:

'The worldwide Occupy movement would like to deny that we have had any part in the recent deaths of people what was being Santa. Although we are completely against the destructive Capitalist System, of which Christmas has become the defining symbol, we condemn utterly the murders of ordinary working-class people what was just trying to earn a few extra bob for their hard-up families, what have probably been shafted by the system, like we all have, apart from the Tory toffs of course. The blokes playing Santa were sadly misguided, but nevertheless did not deserve to die in the horrible ways they have done. If this has been done by anyone in our movement, he or she is a lone wolf, and nuffink to do with the aims of the movement. We advise all other Santas to lay down their beards and come and join us. Together we can destroy this selfish system. Warning: smoking causes lung cancer. Oh sorry, that wasn't part of it. Broadcast this to the world please, Mr BBC man.'

The reporter, who appeared to be in a park somewhere, tried to ask Mr Wilkes a supplementary question; but the erstwhile revolutionary's phone then rang, he answered it, and was heard to say: 'Yes Mum, that was me! On telly! Well I have to talk like that, or they'll think I'm posh. Sorry! Yes I'll be round for Sunday lunch – I'm on my way now…' as he rushed back to the bosom of the proletariat.

Well, well, thought P.; *it must be getting serious when a quasi-revolutionary misses his Sunday dinner to go on the Babylon BBC*. But more was to come…fighting against her throbbing head she went into her tiny kitchen, made another cup of herbal tea (ginseng this time) and returned to bed, wobbling in her long nightie, with a packet of Jaffa Cakes. God how small they are these days! We now seemed to have switched to Afghanistan, as a bearded man looking very like a member of the Taliban was talking to camera. A sporadic translation was being given to his Pashto words:

'We in the Taliban – the true government of Afghanistan, and soon to be in Pakistan…which country is an Imperialist creation…Pakistan that is, not our native Afghanistan…which used to be an Empire itself actually, in the good old days…I bet you didn't know that, did you?… Your Western infidel school books didn't tell you that, did they?…No, I bet they didn't…you probably think history started in 55 BC!…Oh , and don't get me started on B bloody C!…Now where was I?…Oh, yes; we acknowledge the…martyrdom…of hundreds of men with righteous beards…shame about the colour though…of the beards, that is…in the Second Greatest Satan…I'm talking Great Britain, uh – Dude? Friend? Pal? Mate?…Although as far as I can see there's nothing much "Great" about it…you haven't even got any good football teams now!…And watch us whip your ass at cricket in the next World Cup!…Oh I suppose that is one OK thing you have given the world…hardly a reason to call your bloody country "Great" though, is it?…Mmm…you've always been a bit arrogant, haven't you?…Thinking you invented everything… give me a BMW over a Rolls Royce any day!…Sorry, rambling again… anyway, we say that these thousands of murders show the decadence of the Western way of life…that they were perpetrated…ooo, that's a big word, I plucked that out of the ether, didn't I?…without a decent beheading in sight, and no suicide videos at all produced…we in the Taliban would never behave in such a barbaric way…can't speak for those pigs in ISIS, however…right bunch of cunts them lot…if I was you I would look in that direction for a scapegoat…ooo, another good word that…and stop blaming us!

'Long live Father Santa! Death to the Infidel Elves! Come join us for festive reindeer couscous!'

Phaedra was somewhat surprised, but definitely impressed, by the apparent accuracy of the translation, though the bearded Kalashnikov-wielding man on the screen seemed to have stopped talking a while before the translator did. A second later the face of a bespectacled man popped up in the foreground, and said, sotto voce, to camera: 'Translation services supplied by "Larn Yersel Pashto" Productions, Kabul. Simultaneous translations in all the major Central Asian languages supplied. See our website, www.talkforeign.com. Terms and conditions apply.' He smiled, gave a thumbs-up to the viewers, then ducked out of vision; the spokesman was seen to cock his Kalashnikov, before the screen went blank.

Well, well thought P.; *it has become truly international now.* And to think I personally know people involved in it. I could maybe sell my story to the papers – claim to have been Colin's and Harvey's lover – no, thinking about it, I could not stretch the bounds of believability that far. She went back to the papers, vaguely wondering what she would do with the rest of the day; if she ever got up, that is. The thought of Derek and The Phone Call popped into her head again, causing her to chortle out loud. Oh, how sweet her revenge would be; it was just a question of when. She would have to choose her moment with care, when it was most appropriate, and let Derek know exactly what the consequences would be of non-compliance.

The *One O'Clock News* came on; Santa stuff first, of course. A lot of what she had just witnessed was replayed, though not, thankfully, in its entirety: the reverends' row, the Occupy disclaimer, the Taliban denouncement. Someone from the BBC Pashto Service doubted the authenticity of the translation, if not the whole video. Opinions were expressed, a police spokesperson talked a bit but said nothing, various Santas were interviewed, saying it was all terrible, but that they would carry on regardless. In the same vein, the picture now changed to an outside broadcast from the Liverpool Santa Dash, the biggest in the country, which was just about to start. Padded would-be fun-runners were interviewed, all saying that the show must go on, they would not be cowed by the threat of violence, there would be safety in numbers, et cetera. Indeed there would: 8,000 of the estimated 10,000 runners had defied the implied threat. "E can't take on all of us, can 'e?' one jolly entrant said, indicating the mass of red-suited charity joggers. 'Ooever he is. Must be a bloody lunatic, if you ask me. Christmas is t' best time of year, especially for t' kiddies. Why would you want to spoil it? 'E ought to be strung up, when they catch 'im. All the same,' he chuckled, 'I wouldn't want to be one of them stragglers at the end!'

No, thought P., that's not the danger; I know what's going to happen. With a prickling sense of foreboding she fished out her phone, turned it on, and dialled 999. She had never done this before, and did not know what to say; but she had an immoveable feeling that she had to do something.

'Hello? Police? Look, I know what's going to happen on the Santa Run. The one in Liverpool. It's about to start. You've got to stop it! There's going to be a bomb, I'm sure of it…My name? Well – what does that matter? I just know there's going to be…how do I know? Well, I just do! I have a feeling! No, I don't know who's behind it all. I knew a couple of the dead Santas, but that's it. Where am I? In…what does that matter? Just bloody well stop it!'

Then she rang off. It had suddenly become clear to her that they would already have her number, and could easily trace her; and if what she had predicted came true…She half-lay in her untidy bed, transfixed to the (really quite) small screen. The Santas were massed at the start, in front of the 'iconic' Liver Building. Some jolly Scousers had forsaken the traditional red costume for Everton's blue. A big digital clock counted down; it seemed to Phaedra to be in slow motion. She breathed the numbers, along with thousands of onlookers in the Mersey port city. 'Three, two, one, z…' The clock clicked over to zero for a split second –

then a blinding yellow flash consumed the whole screen, followed by an enormous *boom*. Parts of Santas could be seen flying through the air: hats with heads in, sacks with arms attached, boots with legs in. Other bits could have been padding, or real flesh. And then the screaming started; heart- and soul-rending. The camera continued broadcasting; Phaedra could not tear her gaze away. Smoke billowed, the Liver Building was obscured, staggering Santas milled about pointlessly, several limblessly. Sirens then began, adding to the cacophony of chaos. Commentary switched to the BBC Studio; it appeared the outside broadcaster had been injured too.

The cameraman had faithfully carried on filming however, despite whatever injuries he/she may have received. The smoke cleared, revealing a scene reminiscent of the World War One battle recreations on telly earlier in the year; just substitute red for khaki or grey uniforms. At least that partly obscured the huge quantities of blood there must be.

'Fuck!' breathed Phaedra. 'Fucking Hell!' And then her phone rang.

10

Monday, 15 December, was a bright winter day; but the mood in the country could best be described as shell-shocked. It was a bit like the aftermath of the September 11th attacks: everyone in the entire country must have been aware of what had happened, whether they read newspapers, watched TV, listened to radio or not. It was almost too momentous to take in. Casualty numbers were about the 50 killed mark, with many more injured. It must have been a huge bomb, and the explosion was designed to produce the maximum possible casualties. No warning had been received, apart from Phaedra's.

Which of course interested the police enormously. They had phoned her within minutes of the explosion, and were round in less than half an hour, giving their suspect barely time to dress, get rid of the few illegal drugs she had about the place, and hide the more extreme anarchist literature. She did not trust the police, as a good Activist wouldn't, and thought she knew how their minds worked. They were firm but fair, including a policewoman in her escort, and took her down to Greenwich Police Station for 'questioning'. Her links to two of the dead Santas were soon revealed, as was some of her activist past; she was not surprised the Pigs had photos of her at various demos and actions she had been involved in. Even the one with her knockers out from the Internet; a certain amount of eyebrow-raising and winking accompanied that one. Phaedra had been picked up by the fuzz before, at demos, but never kept in and questioned; she was genuinely scared, under her facade of indifference. A lot of what they had on her could point to a possible connection with the perpetrator; alibis proved she could not be the villain herself, but how did she know the bomb was going to go off in Liverpool? It was a bit like the explanation of the solution to a murder mystery, she ruefully reflected. But without a clever detective to do the final reveal. Thinking of which, she did not mention Barry to the detectives at all; not even to Inspector Noel Halliday, who had played 'Good Cop' to Detective Chief Inspector 'Curly' Mudgeon's 'Bad Cop'.

She was released after a couple of hours, told to tell them anything she may subsequently remember which might help them, and left in no doubt that the forces of law and order had her firmly on their radar. When she returned it was obvious her 'flat' had been searched in her absence, very unsubtly. All her anarchist and vaguely political literature had gone, including some old *Class War*s. The Rozzers will love *them*, she thought. She spent a sleepless, turbulent night, visions of exploding Santas filling her dreams. In some she was standing dispassionately amongst the carnage, dressed as an Elf.

So Monday morning found her wandering up The Strand, having got an early train to Charing Cross. She did not know where she was going, but could not stay in the now-tainted flat. The mood was sombre in the extreme, the only noise being made by the newspaper headlines, which screamed murder and carnage to a bruised populace. The thought of Derek in PVC bondage gear did not even raise a mental cheer. She was standing in front of a branch of Ryman's, wondering vaguely if she had any current stationery needs, when her phone bleeped. It made her jump; wow! was she on edge. Looking at the text gingerly, in case it was any more bad news, she felt the blood drain from her face as she read: 'MOF Santa School today cancelled. Please do not go to Abbey Room. Sorry. The Ministers.'

Now the 'MOF' stands for the Ministry of Fun, a loose conglomerate of actors, circus performers, clowns, dancers and the like, who do – well, just about anything they are paid to do: guerrilla advertising, human statues, characters at themed parties, street entertainment, walkabout characters, et cetera. One of their staples is the Santa School, held annually at this time of year, surprisingly enough. They do provide Santas for venues all over the country, but the Santa School is as much publicity stunt for the Ministry as training day for said Santas. It is generally held in the Queen Elizabeth II Conference Centre, nice and central for the nation's media to come and take a peek. Phaedra knew all about it: lots of her fellow murder mystery actors/failed thesps attended, and many played the Red Role, as we have already seen. The Ministry must have tried to text everyone on their contacts list to cancel the event today; but as it was due to begin at 9.00 this was very short notice. With an increasing feeling of dread she turned around and started running towards Charing Cross tube station.

Meanwhile, at said conference centre, all the attendees who had not got the warning, for a variety of acceptable reasons, were bumbling up the steps and following the signs for 'MOF Santa School', in the Abbey Room. All wore the red and white garb; how could it work for publicity photos otherwise? Of course, the recent events dominated conversation, many of the recruits saying they were going to do today's event, primarily out of loyalty to the Ministry, but would not do the actual job, out of…well, fear mostly.

A geeky-looking youth ushered the would-be present givers into the hall-cum-lecture theatre, made sure they were all seated in front of the screen, then told them that James, one of the Ministers, would be with them shortly; in the meantime, he had been asked to show them an information video. With that he turned and walked up the few stairs to the exit, turned on the screen with the remote control, then stepped out of the room. Few attendees noticed him locking the door behind him.

The Santa scholars expected some sort of welcome from James or one of the other Ministers on the big screen; they were all surprised to see a black-balaclava'd face appear, à la IRA. Odd sense of fun, many assumed; must have been shot before the current events occurred.

'YOU are the world's biggest liars,' the face stated, 'every year you, and people like you, perpetrate the biggest conspiracy of untruth on this planet. You are all guilty. Do you feel no shame?'

This was decidedly unfunny; most Santas began to feel slightly uneasy.

'You lie to children, you encourage an orgy of consumerism, you bastardise the meaning of Christmas by encouraging a climate of greed and covetousness. But this will not continue; at least not by you.' Although very uneasy, the Christmas recruits were transfixed by the ferocity of the words emerging from the wool-covered face. Too transfixed to notice a yellowish mist emerge from the heating vents situated around the outside of the room, and slowly roll towards them.

'As a child, I believed vehemently in Father Christmas. It was the most exciting time of the year. It all fitted: the letter sent to Santa, the correct presents arriving, the carrots left out eaten by the reindeer, the glass of sherry drunk by Santa. Why should I not believe? All the evidence was there, and I was a willing dupe. Then my friends at school began to say that he did not exist, and it was all your parents. My parents told me that was not true; I believed them, and kept the faith, despite teasing from my peers. In an effort to strengthen my possibly weakening belief, my grandparents took me to see Santa in Lapland. At the age of 11.'

The first whiffs of the acrid gas began to be noticed around this point, and coughing ensued.

'There I saw the man himself, in his home; I saw reindeer, I saw huskies, I saw snow-covered pine trees – I even saw the fucking Northern Lights. You did a good job; my faith was reinforced, and I returned home convinced – for the next three years!'

By now all the rotund red men were coughing profusely, no longer watching the screen, but climbing over each other in an attempt to get away from the gas. Bulky costumes, sacks and boots made this very difficult, and the survival instinct overrode any festive spirit, as Santas stood on each other in a futile effort to escape. Beards, hats and padding were torn out and thrown off, emerging briefly above then falling back into the all-enveloping yellow fog.

'Can you imagine the merciless ribbing I got from my fellow schoolchildren during those years for still believing, the bullying that ensued, the complete destruction of my self-esteem? Becoming a figure of ridicule, an outcast whom no one talked to for fear of being tainted by his weirdness? And then after all that to finally discover that it was all A FUCKING HUGE LIE?'

None of the desperate throng were watching or listening by this point; besides, the screen had disappeared into the smog. Some made it as far as the door, coughing and retching as they crawled up the steps – to find the only door locked. And on the other side of the strengthened glass partition – the same geeky youth who had welcomed them in, smilingly wanly at them. Their futile gestures for help were met with more smiles and a thumbs-up, as one by one they sank, defeated, into the yellow fog, uncomprehending.

Phaedra raced through the corridors, following the signs to the Abbey Room. She arrived, panting and sweating, outside the soundproof glass partitions – to witness the horrific dumb massacre going on inside. 'Open the door – open the fucking door!' she shrieked to the skinny young lad who appeared to be a member of staff there.

'Oh no miss, we're not allowed to do that – strict instructions: they're doing some kind of emergency training inside, we've been told not to let them out till it's all over!'

Phaedra looked closer at what was playing out inside the room – that could not be right, surely? It all looked too real, and she knew most of this lot were mediocre actors at best. She turned to speak to the youth again – to find he was no longer there. An agonised bearded face appealed to her from behind the glass, white-gloved hand pathetically scrabbling at the door handle. She decided; took a few steps back; then charged at the door, hitting it with her shoulder with all the force she could muster. And she was a strong woman, with no little mass. There could have been a horrible result, shattered glass, blood and bits of her everywhere; but luckily the door just flew off its hinges, Phaedra landing on top of it, to give the *coup de grâce* to that suffocating Santa underneath. She threw the broken door off him, grabbed the white hand, and struggled to pull its owner into the corridor, coughing and spluttering in the deadly fumes. She finally got the majority of the body out into the cleaner air; his red hat fell off, he opened his eyes, looked directly at Phaedra, then coughed his last breaths, which sounded horribly like a version of 'Ho-ho-ho!' Then he died. Phaedra gingerly pulled the white beard off, one hand over her mouth to try to keep out the gas. It was Derek.

11

Things quickly spiralled down out of control after that. The police found Terence's video after the Santa School Massacre, but gleaned little from it. None of the 81 would-be trainees survived the deadly gas, which had been introduced into the heating system, of that room only, earlier in the morning, by someone who witnesses said looked like a caretaker. The venue promised to tighten up their security afterwards: door, bolted, horse. Phaedra, realising how bad her appearance at the event would look in the eyes of Plod, made herself scarce as soon as she ascertained that nothing could be done for the suffocated Santas. Her sweaty dash to the hall had been noticed by some staff however, and it would probably not take too long for even the dullest minds in Scotland Yard to connect the Greenwich Anarchist with that desperate dasher. But in her mind the most important question was: who was the spotty youth who had told her about the survival exercise, and to keep the door locked? She was pretty sure the Ministry would not have done anything like that, confirmed by a quick call to Chantelle in their office. They, of course, were very interested in why she had been there, not being a trainee Santa; luckily they trusted her enough to believe her explanation, and promised not to say anything about her part in it to the police. For now, anyway. None of the other staff she spoke to at the Conference Centre had been told about the survival exercise and locked door instruction either. So spotty geeky boy *must* have had something to do with it.

She found herself pretty much on the run after that; didn't want to go home, because it was bound to be under police surveillance, and didn't want to speak to them for fear of being detained as a suspect. Though she did toy with the idea of giving them information about the loitering geek anonymously. She turned off her phone, having heard somewhere that the Old Bill could pinpoint where you are from the signal your phone is constantly emitting. It is amazing how lost and alone one feels without a mobile phone these days. Not really knowing what to do, but feeling she had to try and find the identity of Geeky Youth, but not having any idea how to go about that whilst 'undercover', she wandered to the nearby Victoria Station, vaguely thinking of throwing herself on the mercy of Saturday night's reindeer, who knew virtually nothing about her, and lived in Sydenham, South London. There was a similar situation in the *Day of the Jackal* film, where Edward Fox's character was trying to remain undercover, she remembered.

The later editions of the *Standard* were, of course, full of the recent, very local, events; Phaedra ignored them, mulling over what she should do next. There is a giant video screen above the ticket barriers at Victoria, which continually spews out news, share prices, et cetera; the stuff users of that particular station are ostensibly interested in. She could not help her eye being drawn to the giant moving pictures; human nature, she supposed. But it was the scrolling words under the pictures that arrested her this time, the breaking news: *Bomb at Macy's kills Santa, 3 Elves, 2 Reindeer, 4 Little Helpers, unknown number of public.*

She was transfixed, as, gradually, was everyone on the station concourse once they noticed the news. A slow gasp went round the hundreds present; apart from those who did not speak or read English of course, who carried on with whatever they were doing. The newsflash kept scrolling round, new numbers being added steadily: 7, 15, 19, 23 shoppers dead. And then the screen went over to live footage: very reminiscent of yesterday in Liverpool, just differently dressed emergency services. *And much better facilities for Santa and helpers*, Phaedra thought; Americans always know how to do things properly. People stayed on the concourse, completely immersed; trains went off to suburban destinations almost empty. Travellers arriving at the station with specific trains to catch, and perhaps not seeing the unfolding video drama, got angry as they tried to push their way through the stationary throng. As did those non-English speakers. Commuters being pushed out of the way got equally angry, voices were raised, people were pushed over, some retaliated, and soon there was a virtual riot going on, brollies and handbags being wielded with apparent relish. The sheer pressure of human beings pushing towards the ticket barriers became almost intolerable, as more and more passengers entered the station, reminding Phaedra of what she assumed the Hillsborough disaster must have been like.

The station authorities tried to intervene, with announcements asking people to leave the concourse; British Transport Police tried to wade in, but could do nothing against the human tide, apart from perhaps making it angrier. Phaedra, thinking of Hillsborough, realised that she was in some physical danger, and managed to climb on to the roof of the small Caffè Nero stand. The terrified staff therein, all Eastern European, were giving away free coffee to try and calm down the throng; very commendable, thought P. They must have their equivalent of the Dunkirk Spirit. Pity I can't use my Caffè Nero loyalty card; I think I am due a free one anyway. And then it happened: a (presumably) drunk office worker, or one with the most inappropriate sense of humour in the world, who had been watching events from the balcony of the first-floor bar in the middle of the station, leaned over said balcony and roared to the throng, at the top of his voice, 'There's a bomb in the station! Gerrout everyone! There's a bomb!'

All heads turned to him, at least those who could hear above the tumult; and the man had a very loud voice, credit where it is due. He was gesticulating wildly towards the exits; so that, logically, is where those who heard him tried to run. Those who had not heard him were of course in the way; the groups collided; the atmosphere of heightened tension made everything seem more dangerous and desperate, and soon the station was filled with a shrieking, screaming mob, all trying to get – well, anywhere but where they were now. Phaedra watched in horror as once again survival instincts overcame generosity to one's fellow man, in their efforts to escape the erstwhile bomb; people were trodden on, children and elderly people especially, people fought each other to protect their loved ones, and the scene became complete carnage. Trampled bodies, some dead and some injured, were everywhere; the Transport Police did their best to restore order, but it was like a pea-shooter trying to stop a tank. Luckily for P., no one tried to join her on the Caffè Nero roof; the pervading direction of travel was away from her. Even the cafe staff fled. Meanwhile, other drinkers on the balcony bar rounded on the culprit furiously, and in a demonstration of justifiable anger threw him over the railings to the floor below. They and the man's friends then started fighting, and several others joined him on the concourse, some dead, others just mutilated. And meanwhile the giant screen showed images of the Macy's carnage, mirroring what was happening for real a few feet below it.

Fucking hell! thought Phaedra, surveying the hellish scene. *What is happening to us? What has this psychopath unleashed?* This was some kind of Dantesque vision of Armageddon; but no one surely, not even the most imaginative sci-fi writer, would have dreamed up Santa Claus as the reason behind it all. She got down from the roof and did what she could for the nearest surviving bodies; but she knew little of first aid, so her usefulness was limited. Sirens raged outside, emergency services poured in, bodies were taken away on stretchers. Some ambulances drove right on to the concourse. Phaedra used scarves, bits torn from her skirt, et cetera to try to stem bleeding wounds, racking her brain to remember the little medical knowledge she had acquired from her time in the Guides, all those years ago. At least it was something; for the first time ever she silently thanked Someone for her middle-class upbringing. She eventually teamed up with a St John's crew, carrying out whatever instructions she was given without question. Made a change for her.

By evening the station was quiet; all bodies, dead and living, had been removed, the station was of course closed, and staff were now mopping up the blood. Phaedra and her St John's crew, Steve and Dawn, had become lifelong friends; a chink of light emanating from this sea of darkness. She had found the man who had cried wolf: he appeared to be alive, but unable to move or even speak. Some would say he deserved it, she mused. But Phaedra did not believe in a vengeful God, and said nothing to anyone about his identity. Others might possibly identify him, but she felt complete paralysis and everlasting guilt was probably punishment enough. The place was now crawling with police, but she managed to avoid being questioned about her part in the disaster until the trains started running again, and she got one to Hayward's Heath, where she had been brought up, and her parents still lived. It was the only place to go now. She sat in the almost empty carriage, and thought of what she had witnessed in the last two days. And then she cried. And cried, and cried, and cried.

12

Could things get any worse? Oh yes, they could! (To bastardise a seasonal pantomimic phrase.) Next day a Santa parachuting into Phuket in Thailand, a traditional treat for the western Christmas visitors, just plummeted straight to the ground, chute having been tampered with. His padding absorbed some of the impact, but not enough. Local kids were seen looting from his sack, trying on his hat and throwing his beard to each other; police fired shots into the air to chase them off. Then Islamist terrorists, or someone like that, wanting to get in on the act, machine-gunned one of the few remaining present-givers at the resort of Sharm-el-Sheikh, in Egypt, plus many western tourists defiantly waiting to receive his gifts. Many birds with one stone, it would seem.

Police all over the planet were now involved; this was unheralded. It could not possibly be the work of one person – could it? Was it an organisation? Or several? Linked, or not? Or were some just copycat killings, using Santa as an excuse to further their own agendas? Or even just for the hell of it, as in American school shooting sprees? Anyone with an axe to grind – or bomb, machine gun, knife even – perhaps felt they could have a go at the Kindest Man in the World. It was incredible – from Most Loved to Most Murdered in less than two weeks! The world had indeed been turned upside down.

The country felt under siege, as the days slipped slowly by towards the big one – 25 December. Lefty social workers appeared on the interminable news shows, saying the anger against the Capitalist system was understandable and inevitable, forcing every known left-wing organisation to deny that they had had any involvement. Even John Wilkes tore himself away from Sunday dinner to issue a much less dialectical denial from the Occupy movement. Across the Pond – which was, of course, now as involved in the crisis as anyone, the Macy's attack being the biggest loss of life in a terrorist event since 11/9 – various members of the more extreme Christian groups to be found in the Land of the Free agreed with the Lefty analysis, but for different reasons. To them this was obviously God's judgement on men who had turned away from Him, to worship Mammon instead. The perpetrators were therefore possibly of supernatural origin, maybe Avenging Angels? And the vengeance was likely to increase, till mankind renounced its wicked ways, and returned to the purity of Christ's teachings. This struck a resonant chord with many people, even those without religious belief; had we not become far more acquisitive latterly, and lost the real meaning of Christmas, whatever that might be? However, the Avenging Angels hypothesis was possibly taking the necessary readjustment a bit far.

And for a while at least the vengeance hypothesis seemed to be correct, from whichever source it came, as attacks on Santas – or sometimes even just men with white beards – continued, all over the world. The Israeli Government, the usual scapegoat for anything wrong in the world, even felt compelled to deny that they had anything to do with the Clausean Cleansing Policy. Fingers in the Arab World had of course been pointing at them for some time, for reasons best known to themselves; and conspiracy theorists had noted that no Santa attacks seemed to have taken place in the Holy Land itself. Sharper minds might have noted that there were no red-garbed colossi in the Jewish nation at that time anyway. Back in Britain, the always-kick-a-man-when-he's-down mob mentality seemed to prevail, as white-bearded, white-haired or even just fat men were abused in the street, the real thing being almost impossible to find by now. It was quite unfathomable, like the anti-paedophile riots in Portsmouth and other places a few years ago; as if the Santa attacks were somehow proof enough of some kind of guilt, be it paedophilia, greed, or – well, God knows what! But once established as a victim, it is very hard to escape that tag.

Shops all over the country removed their Clauses, some compensating them for loss of earnings, some not. Lawyers would make a few bob out of litigation in the New Year. But some parents, those with Battle of Britain blood in their veins, protested about this surrender to terrorism, and tried to force shops to reinstate the Round Red One; others protested about their protests, and violent encounters took place in several of the country's now much emptier shopping centres. Windows were smashed and shops looted in the process. Some Santas stubbornly carried on, hoping to earn the sobriquet of the 'Last Santa in the World', which several of the newspapers were running. They were supported and abused in equal measure on social media. All inflatable, plastic and decorative representations of the man from the North Pole/Lapland were taken down from shops, public buildings, et cetera; town centres became less bright and Christmassy. Officials agonised over whether reindeer and Elves should be removed too; some took down almost every Christmas decoration, others only the Big Man himself. It all looked very odd, compared to a mere two weeks ago.

Even the cinema did not escape the purge. All Santa films were withdrawn, even ones with no direct appearance by Mr Claus in them: *It's a Wonderful Life*, *Nativity x*, et cetera. Television likewise. British and American Equity, their actors' unions, protested against this surrender to violence; notable actors involved in these films made impassioned public speeches in defence of their artistic freedom, under the delusion that it was important to the world. In Paris a group of journalists and actors appeared on TV with the logo 'Je suis Santa' on their shirts and polo-necked jumpers; but none did so in public. In LA, little Dudley Moore was assassinated by an unknown lone gunman for his pains. Someone claiming to be a Peter Cook fan admitted responsibility on the Internet; he was questioned by British police, but released after also claiming to have killed several other actors, some of whom were still alive. Though with some it was hard to tell.

The usual Christmas party season was equally affected; people going to fancy dress dos as Mr Christmas or anything vaguely related to him were abused or even attacked by self-righteous drunks. The heights of black comedy or bad taste (often interchangeable) were scaled by costumes incorporating injuries, lost limbs, et cetera. Even Prince Harry did not stoop that low. National leaders, including both Obama and Cameron, appealed for calm, and that no retaliatory gestures should be undertaken; but obvious non-Christians were already being attacked in the streets by vigilantes – more so in America, it must be said. The Scandinavian countries and Finland, in a magnanimous gesture, offered sanctuary to any Santa or ex-Santa who felt under threat; several took up the offer, but travelled to the airport in disguise. Once there they were met by counsellors dressed as Elves; oh, those ironic Vikings.

Barbers were snowed under (ha!) with men having their white beards shaved off; even white goatees were seen as suspect. With some justification, it must be said. Unscrupulous trimmers, following the laws of supply and demand, charged twice as much for white beards as any other colour. White-haired men dyed it or shaved it off; fat men dieted furiously. Perhaps a silver lining to the whole sorry affair? In towns, villages and cities across the country, people who had previously been proud of their ostentatious Christmas light display took them down from their houses; others left them up in shows of the Bulldog Spirit. But vigilante groups tore some down; homeowners resisted, and more violence ensued. Sometimes the opposite happened: people taking down their lights were abused as cowards by passers-by, and forced to reinstate the display.

At Pudsey in West Yorkshire, crowds of pro- and anti-Santaists gathered in front of a house well-known for its incredible light display;

they usually raised money for charity from viewers, and bus parties even visited. The owner, being a Yorkshireman, dug his heels in, and refused to compromise; this particular night he and family stood in front of their property with cricket bats in hand. The delights of social media enabled a big crowd of each side to gather; chants of 'Gerrem down!' and 'Keep em up!' were exchanged, later degenerating to 'Paedos!' and 'If you're proud to like Santa, clap your hands!' The local bobby radioed for reinforcements to keep the peace; before that could happen a more hot-blooded vigilante, or maybe someone just showing off, jumped over the low garden wall and ran towards the house. Perhaps dazzled by the galaxy of lights he was approaching, the intruder did not notice the 10-year-old daughter of the house run to cut him off, and fetch him a resounding blow to the face with her adult-sized bat. Both sides gasped as blood and teeth were showered in silhouette, and the youth went down like a dropped Santa's sack.

There was a moment's silence; then, as they say, 'all hell' et cetera. Both sets of 'fans' stormed into the garden, fighting with each other, the homeowners, the police, the electric reindeer, whatever. Elves were torn apart in the melee, people electrocuted, windows smashed, strings of lights involved in elongated tugs of war. Riot squads eventually arrived, laying into everyone, and reinforcements for both sides. A helicopter winched the besieged family to safety, the owner grabbing the last remaining Santa from the roof as he almost went down with the sinking ship. News crews arrived, and beamed the whole sorry episode around the world; ah, those reserved English! The police finally managed to separate the gangs, but not before the house erupted in flames, and every single electric light was broken. So the Antis won in that respect; but not necessarily in terms of casualties. Years of cricket practice, starting young, had paid off; even the great Geoffrey Boycott would have approved of some of the defensive strokes displayed by the home side.

13

By Monday, 22 December, the economy and social fabric of the western world was in tatters, especially the English-speaking portion of it. No one had been shopping on the High Street for a week; fear of all sorts of things kept them away. Local shops were doing well, but for the big retailers it was a complete disaster. They generally expected to do huge volumes of business in the Christmas period, and plan their year accordingly; now this was not happening, their economic forecasts were useless. Prices were slashed, food rotted on shelves, staff were laid off. Some reversed their usual policies, and gave away food to the homeless at the end of the day. Never have the unhoused population eaten so well; some people with roofs over their heads pretended to be rough sleepers, to join in the bounty. Some recipients tried to sell it on in more affluent parts of their towns. City centres were deserted as everyone stayed at home; pubs, restaurants, et cetera also had to lay off staff, some closing, never to re-open. Mail order and Internet services flourished, but town centres died, becoming virtually no-go areas. The security industry was the only one expanding. Police were told to look out for looters, as shops closed and were boarded up; some American towns called out the National Guard, and curfews were imposed.

Shares in all the big retailers plummeted, as did those in the entertainment sector. People feigned illness and stayed away from work; productivity slumped, the stock market got the jitters, and a recession similar to that of 2008 set in. Fear and panic gripped the so-called developed world. Asia and Africa were not so affected, Santa not being such a big thing there; but no one could avoid the worldwide economic downturn these events caused. Politicians seemed powerless to do anything; they could not even blame each other for the crisis, although some of course did. As for the military – absolutely nothing they could do against a threat like this. MI5 had been caught completely flat-footed, concentrating on Muslim extremism rather than threats to a mythical being. Easy mistake to make.

The English Defence League had no such dilemmas; they knew exactly where the blame lay. They organised a march in Oldham, to a house destroyed in a Christmas lights attack, close to a predominantly Muslim area of the town. The culprits were obviously close at hand. They got a good turn-out, but banners and slogans were more problematic: as well as the usual Union Jacks there were flags with pictures of jolly Santas, reindeer and sleighs. One young thugette held aloft an old poster for the film *Elf*. Banners proclaimed 'Save Santa!', 'I believe in Cristmas', 'Santa is British' and even 'White Beards Good, Black Beards Bad'. Orwell himself would have been proud.

The police of course were there in force, as always; made a change from defending tastelessly decorated houses. A counter-demonstration from the Muslim side was planned, and with the heightened sense of tension in the air, trouble was widely expected. The EDL, one of whose banners also read 'Santa Defence League', marched up and down past the burnt-out house, a few worried locals watching from their windows and doorways. 'Save our Santa!' seemed to be the main chant; after a while they got bored of just passing the house, and veered in the direction of the police cordon. The counter-demonstration had been steadily mounting, and also veered towards the cordon. Police lines braced themselves; hands gripped truncheons more securely. The Muslim banners were difficult to read from the EDL/SDL side, but were assumed to be anti-British and probably anti-Christian. The Santa supporters stopped at the police lines, and for a moment their chanting stopped, as they tried to read their opponents' messages. Then a voice shouted out from the Muslim side: 'We like Santa too!'

All the SDL supporters heard it; but none believed it. After a few seconds they replied with the ubiquitous football chant, 'You what, you what, you what you what you what?' Never had it been so apt. The Muslims took a few seconds to consider their reply; then came back with, in football chant stylee, 'We like Santa too, we like Santa too, we like Santa, we like Santa, we like Santa too!' The SDL/EDL were completely disarmed by this; individuals approached the cordon, which was still very much braced, and shouted at individuals on the other side. 'What do you mean?' 'Wha-wha-is that true?' 'Do you really like Santa?' were just some of the deep questions posed. Some of their opponents approached as near to the cordon as they could from their side, and actual conversations ensued. The cordon allowed itself to relax a bit; hands dropped from truncheons. It appeared that several on the Pakistani/ Muslim side had actually dyed their beards white, in sympathy with the beleaguered present-giver, and lots of their banners were in praise of the mythical figure! Conversations between participants slowly made it clear that Santa Claus is not an official part of any religion, therefore there is no reason for Muslims to dislike him. This was a revelation to many of the SDL; they seemed to believe he was some sort of Christian deity, as many do. Handshakes occurred across the cordon, and with the police themselves; it was the 1914 Christmas truce all over again, exactly a hundred years on. Everyone wished each other a Happy Christmas; Muslims are quite happy to see others practising their own faiths. And everyone agreed that giving presents is intrinsically a Good Thing.

But that was one of the few Good Things that came out of this bizarre period of British history. Lots of cinemas had closed, whether showing seasonal films or not; all pantos had of course been cancelled, the death of Wishy Washy in Frinton-on-Sea, found dead with a toilet brush up his anus, bristles first, being the final straw. The very words 'Santa Claus' stopped being used; if necessary the being was described as 'Father Christmas'. A bit like Voldemort in *Harry Potter*. Feminists of course used the term 'Mother Christmas', and increasingly 'Solstice Mother', to distance themselves from the now-hated Fat Red One as much as possible. Various types of pagans came out of the woodwork, extolling their fellow Angles, Saxons, Jutes and Britons to jettison the quasi-Christian festival, and rediscover the joys of Solstice mistletoe worship, et cetera. They did enjoy a temporary spike in popularity, until converts realised that naked dancing in the snow was pretty much de rigueur. For everyone. A leader of the Atheist Society appeared on *Question Time*, claiming that the whole thing was our own fault, for raising He Who Shall Not Be Named into a god-like figure; the rejection of all gods was the obvious answer.

On the other hand, at about this time a member of the First Reformed Anabaptist Zionist Chapel, a Protestant splinter group from Utah, USA, congregation numbering 27, admitted on an American chat show that he had carried out all the American attacks, and planned the others around the world. Blessed with the name of Jehosephat Ezekiel Job, he had acted on direct orders from above, it being revealed to him that SANTA was a clever anagram of SATAN. He had no qualms whatsoever about the deaths he had caused. This created a certain amount of controversy on the programme, and within minutes of the show ending he was arrested by the FBI, to join the 53 other apparent homicidal maniacs who had also confessed to the deeds. Jehosephat just did it a bit more publicly. Most were released without charge; some served short prison sentences for wasting police time, and a few were put into the care of state mental asylums. Not a nice fate for any egomaniac. But, this being America, a few were probably genuine.

Football fans at this time of year often wear fancy dress to games, the red and white Gift Giver being the usual choice, especially if that coincided with your team's colours. But this year, instead of mirth, this attracted a violent response from opposition fans, and groups of Santas had to be given police escorts to and from games. Football fans are by and large a reactionary, conservative (with a small 'c') group, so many thought they should not be intimidated by the current apparent anti-Christmas sentiment; whilst for others it provided a justification to attack their rivals. At a Manchester United–Chelsea game, spectators were presented with the spectacle of a group of red and white Santas throwing bricks at a group of blue and white Santas walking towards Old Trafford. The bricks were returned with alacrity. Normally-dressed fans let them get on with it, being unsure of how to react in the current climate.

All the British Santas in Finnish Lapland, of which there were many, were withdrawn in this week, apart from those who accepted the offer of sanctuary. They received a military escort from their various 'cabins' to Rovaniemi, the provincial capital and Official Santa Airport. Once there, they were loaded on to a specially chartered plane, still under military protection, and then given a fighter escort till over Swedish territory, where that country's redoubtable Grippen fighters took over for the rest of the flight to RAF Brize Norton. The three governments bickered over who should foot the bill for years afterwards; the British position was that as Santa was a non-state specific, international figure, no single government should be responsible for his protection, but instead it should be a matter for the UN. Or UNESCO. Or the World Health Organisation. Anyone but us.

Of course the PC brigade loved this apparent rejection of Capitalism and Christianity, the twin evils of the world; *The Guardian* started referring to the 'Solstice Season' and 'Winterfest Holidays'. Scotland re-emphasised its traditional preference for Hogmanay rather than Christmas; it reminded the rest of the still-United Kingdom that Boxing Day only became an official holiday north of the border in 1974. The SNP in particular ranted on about this, in its bid to prove moral and intellectual superiority over 'The English', whoever they were. Elderly members of the Free Presbyterian Church reminisced in newspaper articles about removing Christmas trees from schools in the Highlands in the old days, and not observing Christmas at all, because it was at heart a pagan festival; but getting completely bladdered six days later at Hogmanay was alright in God's book. The mental gymnastics involved were indeed admirable.

Churches in general increased their congregations, as people attempted to find the Real Meaning of Christmas; garish billboards outside several places of worship announced: 'What has been missing from ******mas? Christ has! Come in and find Him!' One risqué establishment in Chipping Norton pushed sensibilities by claiming: 'CLAUS for celebration? Come in and find the real gift of Christmas!' Whilst of course stopping short of praising the current events, many ministers sermonised that perhaps this was a sign that we should abandon the overly consumerist attitudes prevalent, and return to a simpler, less materialistic way of life. This sentiment was echoed by many, many people, for a host of reasons.

Meanwhile the forces of law and order, under pressure from both government and public, had not been idle. Terence's video from the Santa School had been analysed ad infinitum, and his accent had been narrowed down to an area around Swindon, Wiltshire. Many witnesses came forward reporting what they had seen around the time of the attacks, but most were of little use. Apart from Jenny Telfer in Carlisle that is, who had spoken to a spotty youth she strongly suspected was the culprit, but could not confirm that accent; he had sounded local to her. As indeed he had intended to. She herself was now receiving counselling for her traumatic experience, wracked with guilt that it was *she* who had given Ray (*her* Santa) the poisoned cakes that had caused his sudden, but nevertheless agonising-while-it-lasted, death. No amount of soothing words from friends that it was not her fault, that she could not have known what she was doing, et cetera, could erase her feelings of guilt and shame. Her name had been in the local paper. She had killed Ray Burrows. She would never feel good at Christmas time again. The spotty youth had killed a bit of her as well as his intended victim.

Sightings of 'the caretaker' in both Newcastle and London confirmed the general age and build of the suspect; so the beleaguered detectives saturated the Swindon area with appeals to parents of men aged 18–25, who had taken them to see Santa in Lapland, when their child was 11, between about the years 2000 and 2007. This of course narrowed the search enormously, but it was dependent upon a correct accent analysis, and a hope that the perpetrator still lived in that area, or at least his parents did. Memories of the incorrect assumption that the Yorkshire Ripper came from the Sunderland area, based on a tape received by the police that they thought was genuine in the 1970s, were still strong in the minds of the constabulary.

But this time it worked. Every parent who fulfilled the criteria was shown the video, and asked if they recognised the voice. Terence's mother and father, to their eternal sorrow and complete disbelief, did; they confirmed that his grandparents had taken him to see Father Christmas in Lapland when he was 11, in 2004. Exactly 10 years ago. Further inquiries into his past, with school teachers, fellow pupils, and his few friends, confirmed the bullying and ostracism he had received after that visit, and his subsequent refusal to contemplate the non-existence of Santa. Of course everyone involved now felt guilty, claimed that they were not really involved in the bullying, and downplayed its seriousness; teachers who should have helped claimed they did not realise the extent of his alienation, and that 'We did not have a consistent policy on bullying at that time.' His guilt-ridden parents recalled the day they had told him the truth about Christmas, when he had come home from school bloodied, with torn uniform and one shoe missing, at age 14. In retrospect they dated his change in behaviour from that moment: increased truancy from school, which he left at 16, withdrawal into himself, complete lack of friends, seldom leaving his room, increased reliance on his computers, living in a virtual world. Though they, of a different generation, did not realise the extent of his divorce from the real world. He had got a job in a computer repair shop, whose employees described him as completely withdrawn, weird, geeky – like the rest of them – and a computer genius. This is one type of employment where Geek is Good.

In addition, Terence's parents said they had not seen him for a few weeks – he claimed he had some holiday due, and was going to a sci-fi conference somewhere; he had taken his dad's old car, which he occasionally used, though it was still registered to his father's name. They had seen this as a positive sign, that he might be coming out of his shell a bit, and maybe interacting with some real people! As to where he was now, they had no idea: he had not been in touch for over a week. The vehicle was found a few days later, apparently abandoned, in Skegness. Searches of his room and what computers he had left behind revealed a huge knowledge of chemistry and the causing of explosions, large amounts of hacking into shop databases to get names and duty times of various Santas, and widespread contact with extremist organisations, of varied political hues, all over the world. The Dark Web was as clear as day to this delinquent. His phone had not been used since 14 December, and that was in Liverpool. Coincidence? However, investigating officers were sure he must have another computer with him.

It was quickly ascertained that in the three-week lead-up to Christmas 2004 there were 22 British Santas in Finnish Lapland, of whom 20 were now dead. Most of those singled out for 'appropriate' murders had worked there round about that time: as for the others killed, both here and round the world – the police assumed it must be the work of copycat murderers, others with a similar anti-Santa axe to grind, anti-capitalist groups, the religious right, plain psychopaths – anyone really. It was clear Terence had been responsible for the Santa School Suffocation, but the Liverpool bomb as well? That did not fit into his pattern of targeted, highly individual slayings. Maybe he just got crazier, or more megalomaniacal? Or the sight of so many red-and-white-clad runners, all having a jolly time and Doing Good, had been too much for him, when to his mind Santa had done nothing but Evil?

With the announcement that Terence Wilkinson was the main suspect for the British killings, the press of course went into a feeding frenzy about his background, upbringing, why he had done it, potted psychological fantasies about him, and so forth. His pimply face scowled from every newspaper, magazine, bus stop, train station, Post Office, et cetera in the country. It would surely only be a matter of time before he was caught, with an enormous manhunt after him. Foreign media were equally fascinated, although British police thought he was probably only indirectly linked to overseas operations. The US had their own reservoir of homicidal lunatics itching for a reason to kill someone, particularly now they were not currently at war. People appeared on chat shows claiming that prolonged belief in Santa had ruined their lives as well, some even admitting a tiny bit of admiration for Terence. Geoff from Stoke told the nation that he still had a phobia about white beards, and that he had had to have years of psychotherapy before he could go to see Stoke City again, who play in red and white stripes. A surviving ex-Santa appeared on the Jeremy Kyle Show, in silhouette to protect his identity, saying how guilty he now felt at having lied to so many children, and expressing a hope that in future the Arctic-dwelling present-giver would remain in the realms of the mythical, with no more portly bearded men attempting to portray him as real. An official from the Slimmers Society expressed a hope that any future version of Mr Claus would be a bit less big-boned, more in line with the nation's attempts to halt the slide towards obesity.

14

One of the two surviving 2004 Santas, though unaware of that fact, was currently approaching the Swedish/Finnish border in a bus, at the twin towns of Haparanda (Swedish) and Tornio (Finnish). Barry wished he could have travelled by train; but the two countries have different rail gauges, 4 feet 8 and a half inches and 5 feet respectively, so wheels or carriages used to be changed on the bridge which forms the border. The line is now sadly only used for freight. The two countries have different time zones however, and a different currency. So Barry had the childish excitement of putting his watch back an hour, therefore gaining an extra hour of life, and having to get used to different coins and notes. One of the disappeared pleasures of pre-EU Europe, he mused. To him, the European project was a mixed blessing.

It had taken two days to bus it up here; Barry could have flown, but he preferred to watch the interminable snow-covered forests glide by. And think.

Oh, dear; think, think, think. Never did anyone much good, he felt, except perhaps Archimedes. Or Socrates. Some of those Greeks anyway. Most people didn't have much time for thinking, which was probably a blessing. There are no answers. To the Big Questions anyway. Now pub quizzes, that is a different matter. For a long time now all the roads had been snow-covered, in fact whiteness was all one could see, broken by the occasional frozen lake. But Swedes and Finns just cope with it, and drive appropriately. Britain would have ground to a standstill weeks ago – half the country probably dead from famine by now. It was of course bloody cold, sub-zero all the time; but the buses were modern and comfortable, and Barry had good cold-weather clothes from his work, and his mountaineering days. And daylight had all but disappeared as they neared the Arctic Circle; about four hours of twilight in the middle of the day was as good as it got in these solstice days. Oh how it reminded him of his Santa stint 10 years ago, the first time he had been in such northern latitudes in winter.

The border crossing was barely noticed, and no one was looking for him anyway. Next stop was Rovaniemi, announced as the 'Official Santa Airport' when he had landed there in 2004, with a temperature of -9C, at the time the lowest he had ever experienced. But he had lived through much, much lower since. He thought he would probably stay the night in the town, and travel on to Kemijarvi next day, buses permitting. But he would walk if he had to; in fact he might anyway, to make the whole thing more of a penance.

Was it a penance he was engaged in? Or a pilgrimage? Neither, he felt; more of an exorcism. But his innate Presbyterianism demanded some sort of sacrifice from him anyway, even if only blisters on his feet. No pain, no gain, but in a different context. But why had he let Phaedra's non-appearance 10 years ago ruin his life, for a few years if not for ever? It had not happened with previous break-ups, and God knows there had been enough of them. Maybe because he was still in the first flush of love/lust when it happened, and the abrupt ending, for no reason he could fathom, completely knocked him off balance. Or maybe because there was no period of official mourning when he did not see her, because they constantly worked together after that, and saw each other all the time, driving a knife into his guts whenever he saw her being happy and flirty with others. Which happened a lot. And then of course the multitudinous times when they did get together, he thinking each time would be the start of forever again.... Even now he inwardly shuddered at the memory. Please, never go back there. Metaphorically that is; physically, that was exactly what he was now doing.

Meanwhile, the woman in question had been hunkering down in the bosom of her family home, trying to get over the horror of the things she had witnessed. She possibly never would. Her ageing mum and dad worried about her anyway: insecure job, lack of husband, chaotic lifestyle, et cetera, but now even more so. She never came to see them unprompted these days, and never stayed more than a night, usually only on Christmas Eve. So this current sojourn was quite out of character. Phaedra did not tell them everything, for fear of worrying them even more, but she longed to tell someone, to unburden her soul. But having no one who truly loved or understood her, that was impossible. She told them that she knew several of the Santas who had died, that she had been at the Victoria Station carnage, and had seen other stuff on TV, as they had too. Her parents were as sympathetic and nurturing as they could be, for which she was very grateful. They knew there was more to say, but did not push her, being happy that she had chosen to come back to them for sanctuary, if slightly surprised.

For the first few days, P. could not bear to watch any news on TV, for fear of seeing more of the same; her parents complied. She stayed up in her old room a lot, finding comfort in familiarity, as we all do. Lots of her old dollies, teddies and gonks still lived there. Her caring progenitors even hid their daily paper from her, it being full of the ongoing carnage. But by 23 December she had recovered a bit, and was nursing a hot chocolate and talking to her mother, wrapped in a blanket, dressed in her old nightie (Phaedra, not her mother), nestled in her favourite old threadbare armchair, when she accidentally leaned on the remote and turned the TV on, to a morning magazine/news programme. On such coincidences fate hangs.

'Ooo, let's put that off, shall we, Fi darling?' the soothing mother said, seeing Terence's visage, which she was familiar with from all other media, appear on the screen.

'No, it's OK Mum. Who's that?...oh shit'.

Now, their wayward daughter usually did them the honour of not swearing in front of them, or mentioning her sexual or drinking habits, preserving a facade of decency for everyone's benefit. So the slippage of 'shit', so to speak, was correctly interpreted as a sign of something serious by Mrs Jenkins.

'What's wrong darling? Yes, that's the fellow they think has been doing these awful things, He's...'

'Shush Mum! I'm listening!' her daughter commanded. Sylvia did not like being addressed in that tone by anyone, but bit her tongue in order to placate her clearly troubled offspring.

Phaedra listened intently as Detective Chief Inspector Williams laid out the current theory: the fact that only two Santas from 2004 in Finland were still alive, as far as they knew; and their obvious desire to contact those two as soon as possible. Or any information as to the whereabouts of Terence Wilkinson, of course. She knew who one of them was, and hoped he was safely in Sweden; as to the other.... A long-forgotten memory returned with a jolt. Barry had told her about sharing a room in his ski resort in Finland with a 'spare' Santa, who was used by their employers to fill in for any in the country who were ill, injured, hungover, et cetera; they used to take it in turns to do the early morning child-meeting duties when he was not otherwise occupied. And Barry had told her he was scary, and possibly mentally unhinged. Could this be the other surviving Santa?

'Can I use the computer please Mum?' Phaedra suddenly said. Her mother of course agreed; it was nice to see Fi alert and active again, although a bit worrying that it was the news about Terence that had sparked her activity. She took her to her husband's study, where the ageing machine lived (computer, not husband), surrounded by Post-it notes, manuals, photographs, letters, invoices, et cetera; the paraphernalia of an old-fashioned office.

'I think you turn it on there...oh, you already know what to do. Of course you do. Give us a shout if you need anything; your father is in the shed.'Phaedra could not remember the name of the company Barry had worked for in 2004, or the name of the mad Santa; but she *did* remember the name of the man who had employed him: Tommy Winters. She did not know if it was a real name or not, but had always thought it was appropriate for his line of business. It did not take long to find him on the Internet; he was still using that name, if it wasn't his real one, but no longer engaged in the Santa hire game. Now he seemed to specialise in holidays to theme parks, especially for the elderly. Bit of a niche market, she thought, but obviously one that exists. She noted his company phone number, and sent an e-mail, asking for information about Barry's former roommate; but an immediate reply arrived, informing her that the office was closed till 3 January. There was a phone number, which she tried from the home phone, but again it went straight to an answering machine, with the same message. She still did not dare use her mobile, for fear of detection by the Fuzz; although they now had Terence as main suspect, her elusive behaviour was bound to still be suspicious in their eyes.

What could she do? She felt she had to do something, to try to save that other poor sod, crazy or not.

Terence could not find Barry, surely; she herself had no idea whereabouts in Sweden he was, or even if he was still there. He had cut off all contact when he had fled, did not do Facebook, and she did not know anyone still in touch with him. But as for Mad Bad Santa…she made up her mind.

'Dad, do you mind if I borrow the car for a bit? I just fancy a bit of a drive, to clear my head. Maybe to the Downs, or the sea. But don't worry; not Beachy Head!'

That in answer to her father's quizzical expression when she mentioned the sea; Beachy Head is a nearby infamous suicide spot.

'Oh – well – I suppose so – you didn't need to go out, did you darling?' (That to his wife.)'I won't be long – couple of hours I should think – just to, you know, blow away the cobwebs.''Oh, well, yes, alright then, I think the tank is fairly full. Take care of the old girl though, won't you?'

Phaedra promised that yes, she would take care of the ageing VW Golf; it had been in the family almost as long as she had. She did not particularly like driving, having passed her test relatively late in life; before that motorbikes had been her thing, as much to annoy her horribly middle-class parents as for the 'Born to be Wild' effect. As *liberal* middle-class parents, in politics as well as attitude, they felt they could not say 'no' to their only daughter's wish for two-wheeled freedom, but were secretly pleased when she finally gave up the steel steed and accepted their offer of driving lessons. She had never owned a car, having always lived in cities, and never really needed one; so she took special care reversing the vehicle out of the garage, under the somewhat apprehensive gaze of her parents. But no collisions or stallings occurred, and she gave them a cheery wave as she moved off slowly down the drive.

About an hour and several stallings later, but no scrapes, she pulled into Highfield Industrial Estate, on the outskirts of Eastbourne. She had not lied much to her parents: she had crossed the Downs, and was now by the sea, though she was yet to see it. It took her a while to find the office of 'Your Never Too Old' Holidays; up what looked like a fire escape, to the first floor of a two-storey, long brick building, which also housed a car repair garage, a glass supplier, cake bakery, solid fuel stove suppliers, mobility aid shop, ceramic ornament manufacturers – and those were just the ones with signs big enough to read. A veritable hive of variable industry, she mused. She climbed the stairs and rang the bell. No reply, and there were no lights on. A peep through the letter box confirmed that the office was still a functioning entity, but not for the last few days, judging by the post on the floor.

She asked if anyone knew anything about the business owner at the garage underneath; the mechanics eyed her suspiciously, as if she was an enraged holidaymaker, come to demand her money back. *Surely not, if they knew his target clientele?* she thought, sticking her tits out and utilising Flirty Eyes. It worked; young lads competed to give her the most useful information. He ran the business himself, had not been seen for several days, but did live in Eastbourne, though no one knew where. And she did not even have to tell them why she was asking. Men are so bloody transparent; one of their few charms, she opined to herself.

But how to find where he lived? Local register of companies perhaps? But that would probably just have his office address. She drove gingerly into the town centre – very busy for someone unused to driving! – and managed to find the main library. Parking in a car park nearby, equally gingerly, she did not get a ticket – whether from anarchist leanings or plain ignorance – and bounded into the horrible 1960s concrete edifice. 'Local Information' was the first section she came across; the nice helpful lady there did not have a local business register to hand, but suggested she try the phone directory first. P. had forgotten about that –

who but old people use one of those now, and who but old people have their numbers there? But she gave it a go. There were 15 'Winters' in the Eastbourne region; but, crucially, only one 'T. Winters': 22 Wartling Road, BN22 7PJ. This seemed too good to be true, and could easily be someone else; but she took down the address and phone number, consulted a local map, and made her way to said address in the silvery Golf. For once she was thankful for the car's ubiquitous colour.

The light was beginning to fade as Phaedra brought the car to a halt against the pavement in fairly leafy Wartling Road, a few doors down from Mr T. Winters' abode. Although, as it was the middle of winter, all the leaves were rotting in the gutters rather than being leafy on the branches. She risked phoning him on her mobile; no reply, and no answering machine. Made her doubt she was at the right house. Then she quickly switched off her phone. She got out of Mary (the car, of course), and slowly walked towards his semi-detached bay-windowed 1930s dwelling. Garden could do with a bit of attention. Very weedy drive. Fairly big car parked in drive (she had no idea what). Some slates loose, paint peeling from window frames. Not a very well-loved abode; quite possibly that of a single man. But not a gay man. She walked slowly – but not gingerly – towards the front door; she could see a light on in the hall. But just before she reached the dark red, flaking front door, she realised it was slightly ajar.

Alarm bells jangled within her; she was back on red alert. She rang a bell, which did not seem to work. So she knocked, loudly, and shouted, 'Mr. Winters? Are you in?' She thought she heard a moan in reply, so (gingerly, and with a racing heart) pushed the door open. It creaked on its hinges; classic horror material. But this was real, she kept telling herself. The dim hall light revealed an untidy, badly maintained home, with few of the cosy touches of, say, her parents' abode.

'Mr Winters? Are you at home?' she shouted again, stepping into the scruffy hall. She still did not know if this was the right Mr T. Winters, and why his door had been open. Eastbourne may be a relatively low crime area, but most people would keep their front doors locked, she presumed. This time there was a definite moan in reply, and it seemed to come from a closed white door to her left.

She advanced to said door, as gingerly as you like, knocked softly and said, 'Mr Winters, are you in there? Can I come in?' A series of loud, muffled noises answered her; she could not tell if they signified assent or not. But whatever was happening, whether it was the right Mr Winters or not, something seemed amiss; so, taking a deep breath, our heroine (or not) said, decisively, 'OK Mr Winters, I'm going to come in now, if that's all right,' and pushed the door fully open.

Her mind had already played through a few possible scenarios; but none of them came remotely near the bizarre scene which met her eyes when she switched the light on in what appeared to be the living room. A small, chubby man of about 50, with lots of unkempt black hair, unshaven, was lying on the thick but dirty carpet. His eyes were bulging, and he had a piece of duct tape over his mouth; hence the lack of discernible words. But more strangely, he appeared to be dressed as a fairy, complete with grown-up-sized wings. Even to the extent of what looked like rouge on his cheeks, and lipstick. And where do fairies live, when not doing their stints at the bottom of the garden? At the top of the Christmas tree, of course! Tommy Winters, if indeed it was he, was not bucking the trend: a well-decorated Sitka Spruce, complete with shining lights, was lying on its side, and its top appeared to be inserted up Terry's bloodied bottom.

Phaedra recoiled at the gruesome sight; the poor man must have been in unbearable pain. He had obviously been trying to extract the tree, from the blood on the branches and his hands, but the awkwardness of it and the pain involved must have been too much to bear, and he could have been lying there awaiting rescue – for how long? She knelt beside him, and (gingerly) removed his gag. The man's shrieks were genuinely blood-curdling.

'Are you Tommy Winters?' was the first thing she managed to say, looking into his eyes with pity.

'Yeah – who're you?' he managed to gasp.

'Name's Phaedra – Barry's girlfriend – well, ex – but that's not important. What happened to you?'

'For God's sake phone the bloody ambulance, will you? I've been trying to get to the phone, but it's fucking agony. That fucking bastard!' Tommy was weeping with pain.

Phaedra obviously wanted to help the stricken man, but she also wanted to get as much information out of him as she could before the police arrived, and problems ensued. She had a distinct feeling that time was against them. So she dialled 999 from his phone, gave brief details of their location and the need for an ambulance, then came back to the whimpering fairy. She knew she could do nothing to help him; her Girl Guide medical experience did not include massive internal injuries, possibly fatal. For all she knew he could be bleeding to death; but she did not know how to stem that, and wanted as much information from him as possible before the ambulance arrived. She guessed she had about five minutes.

'What happened, Tommy? Who did this? Is this anything to do with the Santa murders?' She still was not absolutely certain she had the right Tommy Winters, though the evidence pointed in that direction.

'You're Barry's girlfriend? Barry McLeod? One of my Lapland Santas? That's who he's after.' Worst fears realised in one line of dialogue.

'He came here this afternoon – recognised him from the pictures – threatened me with a gun – wanted to know where Barry and Gerald were, the only ones he hadn't got yet – wouldn't tell him – had a gun – threatened to kill me – said he just wanted to talk to them – didn't believe him. Where is that fucking ambulance?'

'It'll be here soon. What did you tell him?' Phaedra was desperate for Tommy to continue; he seemed to be weakening.

'Held gun to my head – did Russian roulette – made me dress as a fucking fairy – brought the costume with him!' Tommy was weeping now. 'Said he wouldn't kill me if I told him – so I did – don't know where Barry is, but Gerald's in Doncaster – have kept in touch, works for me now and then – made me give him his address.' Thank God he didn't know where Barry is, thought P. But who wouldn't blab under that pressure? She desperately wanted that Doncaster address, but Tommy carried on with his tale.

124

'Made me bend over – got that fucking tree – I refused, he shot me through the hand – see?'

Phaedra looked at the proffered mitt – what she had presumed was blood from his backside was actually flowing from an inch-diameter hole in the centre of the poor man's left hand. The Christ-like parallel was obvious.

'So much pain – knew he meant it – did what he said – fucking agony! Maybe better if he had shot me – phone rang – he scarpered – you arrived. You fucking saved me. Where's the fucking ambulance?'

'It'll be here any minute Tommy,' Phaedra tried to reassure the poor man, kneeling and holding his other hand. 'But what is Gerald's address? I've got to warn him.'

'Address book – desk – thank you!' was all Tommy managed to whisper – then he passed out. Phaedra gently let go of the good hand, looked at the nearby messy desk, and bingo! There was the well-worn black book. It was open at the 'N's; Phaedra realised Tommy had not mentioned Gerald's surname. But as she looked closer, she realised a page had been torn out from the place where it was open.

'Fucking shit!' she breathed. Tommy was unconscious, so no more help there; she could hear the siren of the approaching ambulance; she had to get out.

'Good luck Tommy, hope you make it,' she sighed, scooping up the address book, and exited by the back door seconds before the ambulance crew ran in through the front.

15

At this point Mr McLeod, as we now know his surname to be, was getting off the bus in Rovaniemi, after the five-hour trip from Tornio. Same snow, same laden fir trees, same frozen lakes as on the other side of the border; just slightly fewer blonds in Finland. Finns do not classify themselves as Scandinavians: their language is very different from their neighbours to the west, and to the east for that matter (Russia, for the geographically challenged); they are also not overwhelmingly tall and blond like the Nords, but much more diverse in appearance. Rovaniemi is a modern city, and to Barry's mind not very attractive; a lot of it was destroyed by the retreating Germans in 1944. He checked into a (relatively) cheap hotel, then wandered the frozen streets, remembering 10 years ago.

At that time the frozen lake at Kemijarvi – the nearest town to the resort he was Santaing at, Suomu (really Suomutunturi in Finnish, but too hard for stupid Brits to pronounce) – was covered by a thick layer of snow. The ice itself was thick enough to drive vehicles over, so Barry had had no qualms about walking into the centre of it. There he had made a huge heart in the snow, with his boots, and, with great originality, wrote 'PJ' (Phaedra Jenkins) 'L' (loves – duh!) 'BM' (I think you've guessed it – Barry McLeod, of course). He leapt between the letters, so no linking footprints would show in the snow, and was very proud of his masterpiece. Even took some photos of it; but the low angle did not show it off properly. Never mind, his true love would soon be here to see it for herself, and admire his proud confession to the world. Even low-flying aircraft might see it, though not, he supposed, astronauts.

Her non-appearance has already been commented upon; and when Barry later showed her the photo prints (remember them?) she had the gall to point out that he had put the curl of the 'J' the wrong way round, so it looked more like 'PT'. Barry loves physical training. How horribly apposite. His snow graffiti would probably remain there till the lake melted in May, he had supposed; people would marvel at it, and wonder who 'PT' and 'BM' were. But at least it would last longer than their relationship had.

At that very time, 'PT/J' was sitting in Newport Pagnell Services on the M1, drinking a coffee and trying to decide what to do. She had already phoned her mum and dad (on her mobile – public phones were now too difficult to operate), telling them briefly that she was going somewhere in the car, she was sorry but she couldn't tell them where, but not to worry because she would be all right, but could not tell them when she would be back. Oh, and please don't tell the police. This had the reassurance value of a political party leader's promise, so poor Sylvia and David spent the next few days chewing their fingernails and jumping whenever the phone rang. She hated doing this to them, but felt she could not tell them anything, and hoped they would understand when it was all over. Whenever and whatever that might be.

A perusal of Terry's stolen address book found two 'Gerrys', but no 'Gerald'; and none of them lived anywhere near Doncaster. She could only presume that Terence had simply torn out the relevant page and taken it with him. It was the last of the 'N's, the next page being blank, before the 'O's started on the succeeding page. There was one slim chance: if Gerald's name had been written on the page over the blank one, faint indentations could possibly be detected. Possibly. She bought a pencil from the shop, then, very, very gingerly (she did ginger well), shaded over the blank page. Her Girl Guide 'Spy' badge was finally becoming useful. As were the horrible fluorescent lights of the cafe. Most of the page produced nothing decipherable; but right at the end, as she was giving up hope, some letters emerged: G-E-blank-blank-L-D. Must be 'Gerald'; what else could it be? N-U-T-blank-A-L-blank; Gerald Nuttall; sounded vaguely familiar, or was that wishful thinking? But what about the address or phone number? She could not detect enough digits to recover the phone number; but the line above it produced: 12 blank-E-L-L L-blank-blank-E. Bell Lane? Cell Lane? Tell Lane? Well Lane? Even Hell Lane was a possibility! Well, that was enough for P.; she was elated. Someone seemed to be on her side. She joyfully downed the dregs of her latte, and almost skipped out to Mary, who thankfully was still there.

Three hours later, via a visit to Woodall Services and purchase of a Doncaster street map, Mary nosed into Bell Lane. It was ten-to-nine, dark and foggy. *How remarkably poignant*, Phaedra thought. She had discovered a 'Well St', 'Gell Rd', even 'Hell Lane'; but it was a tiny ginnell between two streets, so no house numbers at all. Therefore it had to be Bell Lane, if her detection was to be believed. Again she left the silver Golf a few yards away from number 12, and approached on foot. The street was quiet and deserted, the occasional cat crossing, muted sounds of TVs wafting through the mist. Damp, cold and Northern. The houses were small, brick built, probably in the 1980s. Phaedra focussed on where she assumed number 12 was; she thought she saw a movement in the swirling fog; a cat squealed; she heard receding footsteps. She quickened her own, heartbeat increasing again. Oh, God, surely not again: number 12 opened directly from the street; and once again, the door was ajar. Oh shit.

She rang the bell; this time it worked. The light was already on, and she heard noises inside. Oh God, what was she going to find this time?

'Hello? Is that you, Gerald?' she asked, voice quaking slightly.

'Yeah-hey! Come in, whoever you are! Wass your name, love?'; a slurry, Yorkshire, male voice.

She pushed open the door, finding herself in a small, brightly lit, carpeted hallway. Stairs went steeply up to her left, two doors to her right, soppy pictures on the walls (teddy bears, 'home is where the heart is', et cetera), bright but tatty wallpaper. She had absolutely no idea what to expect, so what she got did not completely surprise her.

A man emerged from the first door, staggering somewhat. He wore grey, shapeless tracksuit-type clothes, stained. He was either shaven-headed or bald, unshaven, gormless smile on his face, unfocussed eyes. He looked decrepit, old, wasted. But he might have only been 40.

'Whoosat? Come in, come in! Wanna drink?'

'Hi. Sorry to bother you, but are you Gerald?'

'Who wansta know? Haaaa! You coming in, or what? Wassyer name?' indicating the open door.

Phaedra felt fairly safe: he looked like a decrepit drunkard, whom she thought she could probably overpower if he got a bit frisky – but it was always a risk to go into a room which she could not see inside. But she was desperate for information, so accepted his offer.

It turned out to be a small living room, mostly occupied by a big TV, manky settee, and the detritus of many days' eating and, in particular, drinking: half-eaten takeaway boxes, loads of lager cans, cider bottles and spirit bottles – all Finnish vodka, she noticed. Gerald, if indeed it was he, collapsed on the settee, fished around in a plastic bag and pulled out a can of Tennent's Super Lager, which he offered to Phaedra.

'Gerrit down yer neck me love! Do I know you?' he tried to focus on her disapproving face.

'I'm Barry's girlfriend – well, ex actually – who was a Santa with you in Lapland 10 years ago. Is that right? Were you in Lapland? Do you know him?'

The man, looking somewhat like a creature from *Lord of the Rings*, now tried harder to focus on her face, spilling lager on his leg in the process, which he did not seem to notice.

'F–F– no, don't tell me – F – Fi – Fi – Phaedra!' he finally exploded, waving a yellowish finger in her face. 'Phaedra! It's you! I'd recognise you anywhere! He told me all about you! You never turned up, did you? He was heartbroken. Never got over it. He made a big heart in the snow for you! You never saw it, did you? He said you had big tits. You've got lovely eyes. Why didn't you come?'

Well, that was confirmation if ever there was – confirmation. Phaedra was completely and utterly taken aback by his mini-tirade. To think he remembered, after all those years, and with that obviously addled brain. Barry must have gone on and on about me – oh, God, don't go there! But it was a huge relief to know Terence had not got to him yet.

'Great guy, Barry. But I hated him. And I loved him. He was so good. Everyone liked him. Bastard. I were glad you didn't turn up. Ruined his perfect world! But I were sorry as well, like,' Gerald continued. Phaedra was increasingly at a loss as to what to say. Gerald was unburdening his soul unprompted. She dreaded what he might say next.

'Did you keep in touch with Barry at all?' she probed. 'Any idea where he is now?'

'That's exactly what that bloke just asked! I said he was probably still on that frozen lake at Kemijarvi, waiting for you! It is 10 years ago, in't it?'

Phaedra's blood seemed to freeze in her veins, though biologically that was unlikely.

'What did you say?' was all she could squeeze out through her suddenly dry mouth.

'Whadda say? Who to?' Gerald looked at her with genuinely confused eyes – or were they actually crossed?

'You said a bloke just came and asked about Barry; who was that?' Hint of desperation in her voice.

'Wha bloke? Oh, the bloke that were just ere? Thigme, you know, been on t' telly like. Seemed alright to me. Young fella. Asked same questions as you – do you know him?'

'Did he ask if you had been a Santa in Lapland 10 years ago?' More insistent now.

'Thass right! He did! Funny that. Why'd he wanna know that?'

'What did you tell him?' Even more insistent.

'I said yes! Of course! It were me and Barry what shared it! Good laugh really. Lorra vodka.'

'So did he ask anything about Barry?' Getting to the top of the insistent scale.

'Thass right! He did! Asked where he were now.'

'AND WHAT DID YOU TELL HIM?' 11 on the scale.

'Alright love, calm down! I said I don't know; but he might be back in Kemijarvi like, where you never turned up. Told him the story, he were interested like. Barry were that kind of bloke, y'know; emotional, bit symbolic, know warramean?'

'Did he say what he was going to do now?' Trying to calm down.

'Said he might go and look him up! Silly bugger. He won't be there. Or will 'e, Phaedra?'

Gerald looked directly at her, suddenly focussed, his eyes brown and – well, red mostly. She felt herself turning red as well, as guilty memories overcame her. Even from 10 years ago, and recalled by the gaze of this derelict drunkard. That annoyed her.

'When was he here then?' she managed to say, brusquely and defensively.

"E left just before you did love. Did you not see 'im? Thought you might be 'im coming back for his bottle!'

'Bottle?? What bottle?' Curious rather than defensive.

"E gave me this!' Gerald replied joyously, holding up a half-full bottle. 'Said it were a Christmas present! Bloody lovely it were too. No idea wharritis, though!'

Phaedra thought she did, and looked closely at exhibit A. Some kind of spirit, she presumed; probably vodka, from his sense of appropriateness; but the label...looked like it had been printed from someone's computer: 'Santa Cull: A Soon-To-Be-Classic Christmas Brew', with images of dead and bleeding Santae. She looked closer; yes, it was a photo from the Liverpool bombing. The bastard had a sick sense of humour. In fact he was just sick, very sick.

It looked like Gerald had already drunk half of it; Terence must have known he was likely to do so.

Any chance of making him sick? A look at the grinning face holding the bottle did not look promising.

'Gerald, mate, I think that was poison,' she tried anyway, attempting to bond with the added 'mate'.

'Yeeeah, it's all poison! That's what you all say, you bloody social workers! Is that what you are, a bloody social worker – or a God botherer! Are you a vicar's daughter? Ha! Well you can fuck off, I'll drink what

I like. Go on, fuck off, out of my house! Barry were better off without you! Back to bloody Sussex!' as he gesticulated wildly towards the door with his Santa Cull.

How does this man know so much about me? thought P. *That is uncanny, even down to the location of Haywards Heath.* But she did not think about it too much, as Mr Nuttall was now living up to his name, shouting and swearing at her, and looking increasingly violent. She obeyed his instructions, ran down the small hall – or was it a vestibule? – and was soon back out in the still foggy street, his ranting mingling with the wafting television sounds.

Now what to do? She *could* just leave the ex-spare-Santa to his fate; it might be too late for him already. She had no idea how quickly various poisons worked, definitely never got her 'Lethal Liquids' badge in Guides. But from the noise coming from the house, he still sounded pretty healthy. Well, not healthy, but alive. She could just leave him, and go and save Barry, however that could be done; but ultimately Gerald was right: she *was* a vicar's daughter, and, buried within her, though not too deeply to be honest, was a motto saying 'Do unto others what you would have them do to you'. Or words to that effect. So, breathing a huge sigh of resignation, she turned on her mobile and dialled 999.

There were a few strange clicks and noises on the line – then a voice answered that sounded familiar.

'Phaedra – is that you? This is Inspector Halliday from Greenwich Police. Remember? We talked a few weeks ago. No, don't hang up; you're not in trouble. We've been worried about you. Are you OK?'

His tone was measured, calming, with just a slight undertone of desperation. Phaedra hesitated, finger poised over the 'off' button; then relented.

'How did you know it was me?' she replied, resignation in her voice.

'We know your number; as soon as you call any police number it will come through to here. We've been looking for you. And look, we know everything now: Terence, Barry, Gerald, the lot...'

'Well you'd better get up here and save Gerald quickly then,' she almost snapped, 'Terence has visited him and he's drunk some poison. 12 Bell Street, Doncaster. Hurry up!'

'Is that where you are? Now look, just stay there, we'll be along as soon as we can...'

'Sorry Inspector, I can't do that. I have to go and save Barry. Just get here quick, and do your best for Gerald. Thank you for caring. Bye.' Phone off; she didn't have time to hang about.

16

24 December, 2014. Christmas Eve. A tall, skinny, fair-haired youth, sporting a rather dashing moustache, stepped down from a Finnair flight at Rovaniemi Airport, Finland, more-or-less on the Arctic Circle. The temperature was -15C, but he was well wrapped up, in thick military greatcoat and Russian Army style fur hat, which helped conceal his face. Very few other people got off the plane, and those that did scuttled quickly off to reclaim their baggage. The youth took his time walking down the steps however, surveying the scene; a smile played on his lips at the sight of the giant 'Official Santa Airport' sign, which formerly adorned the side of the Arrivals terminal, now lying smashed and forlorn on the tarmac. He wanted to drink in the scene, and replace the memory of 10 years ago with this revised scenario. And all happening because of him.

On entering the terminal building he was approached by a young girl dressed all in green, with strange red make-up, pointy ears and a green and red cap on her head. Terence, for it is indeed he, in masterful disguise I am sure you will agree, visibly tensed, knowing what was coming.

'Vellcome to Lapland – uh, Finland sir! Vill you be vanting to claim (winked eye at this point) *political* asylum?'

The blood rushed to Terence's face; long-suppressed fury boiled within him; his hands clenched and unclenched; his moustache twitched strangely. His reply came in staccato bursts, like gunfire.

'No I…do not want…to claim…any sort of…*fucking* asylum!'

He had not wanted to use the f-word with this poor girl, not wanting to draw attention to himself at all; but the memory of seeing just such an 'Elf' 10 years ago, equally badly made-up – how could even *he* have been fooled then? – got the better of his gargantuan self-control. Anything less than gargantuan and he would probably have tried to pull the poor girl's head off, hat and all.

'Sank you for your strong reply sir. Ve haff to ask everyone, as I am sure you vill understand. All zese awesome things' (*she probably meant 'awful'* thought T. *Or did she? Maybe they were on the same side after all?*) 'happening, vot kind of a monster could be doing zat?' and she looked Terence squarely in the face, as though it was not a rhetorical question.

'I don't know, I'm sure,' he mumbled, 'yes, awesome! Em, awful! Yes.'

'Vell Vellcome to Lapland anyvay sir! Have a lovely Christmas! And sir—' this as he was walking past her '—nice moustache!' And another vink.

Thoroughly unnerved once again by this brief exposure to Finland, Terence hurried away, not even noticing the Elf talking into a small radio transmitter she carried in a brown leather pouch. Was he losing his grip? Would his nerve fail him so near to his ultimate goal? He was not sure if 'Barry' would be there or not, of course; but something about what that drunken fool Gerald had said clicked inside him, and he was somehow certain that he would complete his revenge on this of all days, and in this of all places: where the Evil Lie had been perpetuated, and his slide towards social ostracism and eventual psychopathy started. That girl Phaedra who hadn't turned up 10 years ago; the idea of something coming round full circle; it would be perfect if this would be where it all ended, all the loose ends tied up, his life's work done, already! And if 'Barry' wasn't there – well, it would be an appropriate place to be anyway. What he would do then – he had not thought that far ahead.

In fact, Terence was amazed he had got this far; even more amazed by all the mayhem caused by the other Santa slayings around the world, and the end of the Capitalist system that had almost ensued. If only Karl Marx had thought outside the box! Forget seizing the means of production, just kill the bloody present-givers! He had been in touch with other Santa-haters of various political, religious and social hues around the world, but never expected it to reach the crescendo of death it had done. A bit like the 11/9 attacks, he mused. He knew the police had by now identified him; had even seen his poor parents tearfully beg him to stop it all and give himself up, on TV. Well, it was their own fault, making him believe so vehemently in the whole falsehood, and letting his deluded grandparents take him over here, to be even more deluded. So let them suffer, and be social pariahs, as he was for 10 years. History would prove him right, like Hitler; one day he would be thanked for destroying the colossus of lies dedicated to consumerism that was Joulupukki, as he is called in Finland.

To a man of his huge intelligence, disguise and getting past security checks at airports was easy. The forging of passports was something he had been practising in his bedroom lab for several years, in preparation for just such an eventuality. He was even getting quite fond of the blond moustache; very 1970s apparently. He did not think the police had any idea of his whereabouts; no one seemed to know where this Barry was, it was only by chance that Gerald blurted it out; Tommy Winters had had no idea. Terence particularly enjoyed his Christmas tree fun with Mr Winters; he was the main Santa pimp after all, so being arse-fucked by a Christmas tree was a very appropriate way to leave this world. And appropriately painful, he expected. What he would do with Barry when he found him…he had not worked out all the details yet, but his heart on the frozen lake had a nice ring to it, given what Gerald had said about the events there 10 years ago.

And from what Tommy and Gerald had said, he thought that Barry might have been the actual personification of evil he had seen in 2004, at Suomu, which Terence had previously thought was the Finnish name for Finland. As a wide-eyed 11-year-old child, Terence had not known which particular Santa resort his grandparents had taken him to; as far as he was concerned, Santa only had one home, and that of course is where he went. The question of where lots of the other children on the Santa Airlines flight had gone to after arrival in Rovaniemi never entered his amazed head. So when the time came for him to try and discover the identity of the actual

Arch Liar whom he had met in his supposed home, it proved very difficult, with over 20 locations in Finland being used to fleece well-meaning British and Irish parents and grandparents that year. Records had not been kept on computer files anywhere, and even jolly Tommy Winters, playing the fairy on top of the Christmas tree, was unable to tell him for certain which location he had been deceived in. But something Gerald had said about the jerry-built 'Santa hut' he had 'worked' in, apparently finished only hours before the first child arrived, with electric cables still sticking out of pine walls, rang a tiny memory bell in his head. Even more reasons for him to have had doubts – but still he hadn't! He must have been the most trusting child in the world. Or at least in Swindon. Well, the higher the pinnacle of trust destroyed, the greater the reaction to that betrayal. But wherever the awful event had taken place, and whether Barry was the perpetrator or not, to kill him would mean he had eliminated all the culprits from that year; so one of them must be the one who had deceived him. Again. Everything seemed to be rounding itself up nicely.

Back in England, a very tired and almost-at-the-end-of-her-tether Phaedra was observing the check-in desk for the last Finnair flight to Rovaniemi – from Heathrow. Unlike the wily Terence who, armed with prior knowledge, had got the 7 a.m. flight from East Midlands Airport, Phaedra had gone to the nearest departure point of the metal fuel-gobbling environment-crippling monsters – Humberside. To find, of course, that there were no direct flights to Finland. So, throwing caution (and her credit card, which she rarely admitted she even had) to the winds, she had got a very late flight to Heathrow, spent the night in anxious non-sleep on uncomfortable benches, along with the rest of the human jetsam found there at that time, and was now warily scanning the check-in desk for the last flight before Christmas, at 9 a.m. In former glorious days this would have been a joyous flight, the Christmas Special, full of people, including lots of newlyweds strangely enough, off to spend Christmas in the home of the Father of it all, Lapland. But today…very few passengers were approaching the desk, those that did seemed very furtive, and all had the air of scared rabbits. In fact, the entire airport seemed furtive and suspicious – as did most of the country.

But of more concern to the nearly exhausted blond, busty ex-activist and occasional actress was the level of security around that particular gate, not to mention the airport in general. Pigs with horrible-looking guns were everywhere, trying to strut around, but never looking as cool as Americans in movies. I mean films. Is that one of our national traits, she wondered, to always come off second best to the Yanks? Sometimes even third or fourth; French riot police look like they could kick *derrière* in a *très* cool manner. She wondered if her name had been circulated around, despite Inspector Halliday telling her on the phone that they were on her side? But she had to try and get through anyway, no way could she try a disguise at this late stage in the game; when she had left home to go to Eastbourne, what seemed like a lifetime ago now, she had not expected to be attempting to leave the country disguised as someone else. Obviously the Guides' 'be prepared' motto had fallen on deaf ears in this case. Or was it the Scouts? Some well-meaning righteous spirit-uplifting organisation anyway.

So she opted for the 'I'm in a rush, you have to let me through, my plane is just leaving' approach, waiting till there were only about 10 minutes to go till take-off, then dashing at the desk in mock alarm. All her barely-earned acting skills came to the fore; she felt she overdid it a bit, but then so do lots of people. Mostly Americans and the working class. She affected mock-irritation while the Finnair employee checked her passport, whereas in reality her heart was beating like a German oompah band, and sweat ran down her tense back. And then it almost stopped (her heart, that is) when the minor official nodded to the nearby policeman, who looked up at Phaedra – and brought his semi-automatic rifle into the 'ready' position.

'Miss – *Ms* – Jenkins? Would you step over here please?' he said, in a way which brooked no refusal. Phaedra noticed the use of 'would', rather than 'could': much more forceful, whilst appearing to give some choice.

'Why? What have I done? My plane leaves in 10 minutes!' She did not even sound convincing to herself.

'Just step over here please. We'd like a few words with you. This way please.' His tone was becoming firmer by the syllable.

Phaedra's sweat was now over most of her body; and not in a good way. She had never had a gun even vaguely pointed in her direction, let alone one now cocked and beginning to get erect. Things seemed to go in slow motion, or somehow to be happening to someone else. And then she had a brainwave, and reached into her inside pocket for her phone.

'DON'T TOUCH THAT! TAKE YOUR HANDS AWAY FROM YOUR BODY!' that tone was as firm as you could get, likewise his weapon, which was now levelled directly at her; as were about a dozen others, of various shapes and sizes, which suddenly sprouted from men all over the departure lounge, also of all shapes and sizes, some in uniform, some not. Some even women! That seemed extra wrong to Phaedra. They were now the only people standing; everyone else had flung themselves on to the floor, or sought the doubtful protection of tables, chairs, vending machines, et cetera. Phaedra's heart almost stopped, literally and metaphorically; as did her right hand, currently resting on the top of her fairly antiquated Nokia. How appropriate, for a trip to Finland. Do you know they are made there? Well, you do now. She did what she was told, and slowly pulled the object of dubious desire out of her pocket, showing it to the ultra-tense security man, as her other hand reached for the sky. He tensed even more, if that were possible; they all did. The sound of safety catches being snapped off took the place of pins dropping.

'DON'T TOUCH THAT PHONE! PUT IT DOWN ON THE FLOOR! THERE!' and he indicated an area with his rifle, just in front of her, whilst taking a few steps backwards, Phaedra noted with interest. She sensed a change in the balance of power, and imagined herself in the spotlight, delivering the crucial monologue of some very worthy play. At least she would be able to project properly, so everyone would hear what could possibly be her final curtain call.

'I am going to phone Inspector Halliday; he's in charge of this operation, right?' She was looking directly at her interrogator, hoping she sounded surer than she felt, talking slowly and enunciating every syllable, as every actor was formerly taught. For all she knew, Halliday could just be an errand boy, and that might not even be his real name anyway. But, with relief, she saw a flicker of recognition cross Gun Ho's tense features.

'He knows who I am, and he knows I am not the person you want. I have to get to Finland to save the sole surviving Santa.' Brilliant! Alliteration under extreme duress! Wait till her old English teacher heard about this.

'Halliday? Yes, he is one of the DIs involved in Operation Rudolph.' (*Crap name*, thought Phaedra; *these people really have no imagination.*) 'How do you know that?' Gun still trained on her, however.

'He interviewed me a week ago. About this stuff. But he knows it wasn't me; told me last night. Let me phone him, and he will tell you to let me go'. All was still very tense around the 'lounge'; though Phaedra detected a slight thaw. But the clock was still ticking, unfortunately not in slow motion, and the Finnair employee was visibly twitching.

'Yeah, but *we* don't know who you are. If you dial that phone, it could set off a bomb; maybe nowhere near here!' *Well, well, is that right?* thought P. *Tell the world how it's done, why don't you?* 'Why don't *I* dial him, on my phone? Then that can't happen.' He was beaming like a Cheshire cat, proud of his brainwave.

'But no! It's got to be me. My phone number goes straight to him. And I have to get that plane in' (glance at big clock on wall) 'seven minutes!'

'But we don't know if you are who you say you are,' the stubborn guardian dug his heels in.

'Well you can read it on my bloody passport! Look! Phaedra Jenkins!' holding up said object. Gun Ho looked like he was going to place another logical objection in her way; the clock ticked a few more seconds; then salvation came from a completely unexpected angle.

'Phaedra Jenkins? Boobs Not Bombs? Fourth most viewed set of – uh, breasts – on the Internet in July 2005?' one of the surrounding gun-wielding men expostulated. Phaedra stared at him, almost unable to comprehend what had just been said.

'Uh – yeah, that's right. How'd…who're you?'

All heads were now turned in the direction of a tall man who looked every inch a smart, high-powered businessman, from his polished brogues to his gold personalised cufflinks – apart from the fact he was aiming a rather large Luger at the lady he was currently addressing.

'Spectral Steve! Remember me? Tooting Anarchists? We did some GM actions together. Long time ago now,' he added quickly, suddenly aware of the stares of his fellow 'officers', the jaws of several of whom now rested on the synthetic carpet.

'Stevie? Spectral Steve? Is that you? Wh–what happened?' Phaedra expostulated, picking some carpet fluff off her own jaw.

'Yeah, it is me! Look!' and with that the 'businessman' lifted up his shirt and string vest – to reveal silver rings through both nipples, and a huge 'A' in a circle tattooed on his chest. All jaws were now resting comfortably on the slightly stained carpet, and weapons dangled from limp hands.

'That was – uh – a long time ago now, y'see,' he quickly explained. 'I've uh – changed my ideas. Seen the light, so to speak. Sorry, Phaedra. I always liked you. Could you – uh – um – uh – show us your knockers, for old times' sake? Just to prove who you are.' That last bit an afterthought, but a bloody brainwave.

The ludicrousness of the whole situation suddenly hit Phaedra: she holding a shabby, cracked mobile phone in the air, the other hand as high as she could reach, clenching passport, surrounded by a dozen men with sagging guns and even more sagging jaws, looking at a tall, well-dressed businessman currently holding up his shirt and vest to show pierced nipples and an anarchist tattoo. In Heathrow Airport. On Christmas Eve. With five minutes to go before her flight flew. But he was the centre of attention! That couldn't be right. There was only one thing to do, and she did it.

'There you are boys! Oh, and girls! Ten years on, but still worth looking at!'

A lot of male heads nodded their appreciation; and one of the gun-wielding girls too, Phaedra noticed with pleasure, as she held up her woolly jumper, shirt and black bra to reveal her secret pride and joy. She even gave a twirl to the whole lounge. The Finnair employee could be seen talking quietly into a microphone, almost as if he were doing a commentary of the proceedings.

'Yes, that's her alright! Let her make the call, super,' 'Steve' said, whilst still feasting his eyes on those lovely erect pink nipples. Being the centre of attention had always aroused Phaedra; hence the choice of career. She looked at Gun Ho questioningly, who did not really look very super to her; he just nodded his dumbfounded head, whilst focussing on the double bullseyes. She brought the phone down to head height and dialled 999 as fast as her fingers would allow. She was performing now, centre stage, all fear gone, focussing on her primary objective. Her drama teacher would have been proud of her. And still the clock ticked, however inaudibly; four minutes to go.

'Phaedra?'

'Mr – Detective – Inspector – whatever you are, Halliday, yeah?'

'Yes, it's me. Where are you? Wh — ' 'Just listen, *Noel* (she had finally got the reference), I am at Heathrow Airport. Tell your men to let me through. My plane leaves in – four minutes.'

'Where are you going?'

'Finland. Doesn't matter. I hope to see Barry. Terence is still in the country, isn't he?'

'Y–ees, as far as we know he hasn't left these shores…'

'Good. Well, I'm just off to Finland to fulfil a promise I broke ten years ago. Tell them to let me go,' and with that she rang off. She knew they were meant to be on the same side now, but she didn't trust the Rozzers not to cock things up. She felt she was the only one who could save Barry; the only one who *ought* to save him. That is if he was even where she thought he would be, and if Terence was actually after him and knew where he would be too. Might be. Probably wouldn't be. Whatever, only she could do it. Her theatrical romantic heroine complex had taken over completely now.

Then she waited – as did they all, as the clock ticked ever so slowly. Everyone seemed to jump when Gun Ho's radio suddenly squawked: 'ZZt – mzz – let her go, Bob. In fact, escort her to the plane. She's got to get it. Do it now!'

'OK Inspector. Will do. *Any volunteers*?' A touch of sarcasm, tinged with having been overruled, pervaded Gun Ho's request.

At least 20 hands shot up, some of them from people lying on the floor, who had witnessed the exchange. Phaedra suddenly realised she was still holding her clothes up to her neck, in 'boobs exposed' position. It felt just like the old days.

'Stevie – and that girl there!' Phaedra expostulated, pointing at the girl who seemed to have been admiring her knockers. Keep all options open, she had always opined.

No further asking was required, and they sprinted along the empty corridors towards gate 27, even the Finnair employee accompanying them.

'Yeah, they were good days, eh, Phi? That's what you used to call yourself, wasn't it? Sort of "Phi, Phae, Fo, Fum, I smell the blood of a COR-POR-A-SHUN!" sort of thing. Yeah, great times. Running from the Rozzers, laying down in front of diggers – brilliant,' Stev(ie) chuntered on as they dashed, looking completely wrong in his suit and Luger, which he was still brandishing with some glee. The few people encountered flattened themselves against the walls as they passed, not knowing if gun-waving in this context was a good or bad thing.

'So why this now?' Phaedra managed to get out between pants (of the breath type). Stevie had obviously benefited from the fitness levels expected of his new occupation.

'Well, I thought, if you can't beat 'em, join 'em! 'Coz we never *really* did any good, did we? Only delayed stuff a bit. Soap-dodging protesters never changed public opinion, did we? Just made people more annoyed. So I thought I'd go over to the opposition. MI5 love people like me, to infiltrate – groups' (this said slightly sheepishly and apologetically; Phaedra's mind went quickly over the various high-profile infiltration stories recently in the news). 'Poacher turned gamekeeper, you know?'

I have moved on P. thought, *I object to being described as a soap dodger now!* But before she could continue in her role as Stev/ie's confessor, the smiling Finnair employee pointed to the left, and there were two stewardesses waiting somewhat bemusedly at the aeroplane door.

'Thanks a lot Stevie,' she had time to say, 'see you again sometime!'

'Yeah, look after yourself Phi, there really are some evil people out there. Honestly!' Steve's world view had shifted dramatically during the last 10 years, it seemed; but so, she realised, had hers.

The accompanying policewoman was not so coy, but boldly planted a smacker on Phaedra's full lips, adding, 'You're awesome, babe! Come back to me if you don't find him!' before she was ushered inside the waiting aeroplane by the still bemused hostesses. She saw the Finnair employee blow a kiss at her, and then the doors closed behind her. *What a bloody send-off*, she thought, as she made her way slightly sheepishly down the aisle; *I ought to do this more often. Like maybe every other decade.*

17

Over in Finland, Barry was at that time sitting in a bar in Kemijarvi, the town nearest to where he had done his Santa stint, the ski 'resort' of Suomu. He liked the town; in winter, at least, it was a bit rough-and-ready, like a frontier town in the Rockies he liked to think, with checked-shirted men in fur hats and beards drinking in basic bars, getting pissed and singing. Very like the town of his upbringing, in northern Scotland. Not much posing and trendiness going on here, he was pleased to see; the sub-zero temperatures and pavements snowed over for five months of the year saw to that. High heels or poncey shoes could not cope with that. Though he had nothing against stiletto heels; higher the better.

He had stayed the night in the Hostel Kemijarvi, fairly basic accommodation, but it suited his mood. Ideas of walking from Rovaniemi had been ditched when he had realised how far the towns were apart: 40-

odd miles. With the mere four hours of twilight available, Barry decided his journey was not really a penance. Instead he took the train, the most northerly in Finland, enjoying the vast white forest and innumerable lakes that clanked past the window. Or the other way round.

It was now Christmas Eve, with all the enormous resonances that held both for Barry himself and for at least a third of mankind, he roughly estimated, based on very little hard evidence. It was not the same for the local Finns as in Britain, or America; although Santa is purported to dwell somewhere in the icy northern reaches of their country, they do not make such a fuss about it. Roughly the same number of locals would be getting pissed that night as any other. Barry liked the fact that the Finns liked a drink; reminded him of home. They were also rather partial to saunas, heavy metal music, country and western music, and suicide. At least two of those facets also reminded him of home.

But where was home for Barry now? Sweden? It certainly did not feel like home, more like somewhere he was just passing through, albeit very slowly. But passing through to where? On his way back to Britain, the Scottish Highlands, or another country altogether? He liked Sweden, to a certain extent, but could not see himself settling there. It still felt like he had unfinished business back in Blighty, although he did not know how, when or if he would ever finish it. He had cut off almost all contact with his motherland, but it was always still there, in the back of his mind, like a very, very thin and long piece of elastic, slowly pulling him back in, if he let it. So far he had not let it.

So he drifted round the small town, only about 5,000 population he thought, calling at the bars, having a drink or two, thinking about what happened here 10 years ago, trying to find the bars he had visited then. None of them looked familiar now. After 1 o'clock the already dim light slowly began to fade, and Barry swallowed his last mouthful of Sahti, Finland's traditional, but very odd tasting, beer, slammed the glass on the bar with deliberation, and strode out into the freezing twilight.

If some over-arching, all-seeing being – God is the obvious candidate – had a map with flashing dots on indicating the positions of Barry and Terence, a bit like *Harry Potter*'s marauders' map, or the one in *Alien* indicating the creature and the poor crewman we know is going to get it soon, those dots would now be very close. They were briefly together 10 years ago, drifted apart, by several hundred miles at times, but had recently been getting slowly closer. 'God' would now need a very large scale map (or is it small scale? I'm never sure), because they were actually only a few hundred yards apart, as a very cold crow would fly. Though as we are in Finland I suppose we should use metres, and I don't know if there are any crows in that part of Europe. Whichever: neither of them knew it; only God did. Terence hoped for it, Phaedra feared it, Barry didn't have a clue.

The man who hoped for it had recently arrived from Rovaniemi, using the same train Barry had done, just 24 hours later. Of course he had done his research, and headed straight for Kemijmarvi Lake/Lake Kemijarvi. It was big, very frozen, very indented, full of islands, and surrounded by low forested hills. He knew from Gerald's description that this was the place his mortal enemy had arranged to meet his supposed 'lover' (a term Terence theoretically understood, but had no experience of, at any level). At this very time, and on this very day, exactly 10 years ago. Terence had by now eschewed all knowledge of probability, and convinced himself that Barry was definitely the Vile Villain who had fooled him in that fateful year. If he was going to find him again this was the most likely place, from Gerald's explanations of Barry's character and behaviour. He did not know exactly where the Most Evil Liar had made that heart in the snow, but from where he was now standing he could see a lot of the frozen expanse. He did not think Barry would have gone too far from the shore, either from fear of cracking the ice, or convenience for meeting his amour; but at that moment the lake was completely free of humans. Despite the gathering gloom it would be easy to see anyone venturing on to this natural ice rink, they would stand out stark and black against the all-pervading whiteness. What snow had fallen on the lake was now frozen solid; Barry would find it hard to make his love symbol now. What a godforsaken place to imagine a mythical being to live, Terence thought; if humans are stupid enough to invent another, now I have destroyed this one, I hope they have the intelligence to site his home somewhere else. Hawaii, for example.

The Thorough Assassin had of course prepared himself for the local weather conditions (currently -17C), but even he could not stand still for long without the threat of frostbite on digits becoming reality. So, having assured himself that the lake was devoid of life, above the ice at least, he turned away and walked briskly back towards the nearby streets. His boots were good quality, but not designed for extremely cold conditions, so a certain amount of foot activity was required to prevent the insidious creep of Jill Frost-Bite, Jack's younger but more vicious sister. Same with his gloves; the fact he was also carrying a small bag meant they could not be thrust into the warmth of pockets. He may have been a metaphorically cold person – no, make that frozen – but biologically he was still warm-blooded, and required heat to survive; so he headed into the nearest bar, the Viisiiko Pub. Bar/pub culture was completely alien to Terence, never having consumed alcohol in his life. In fact, culture in general was alien to him. But he needed the warmth, and was intelligent enough to adapt to situations if he had to, as we have already seen.

'God' would now need a very large/small scale map indeed, for those two flashing dots, red for Terence and blue for Barry, had almost merged (which would of course have formed a purple patch): Barry walked out one door of the Viisiiko as Terence walked in the other. Of such unknown coincidences is life made. Or perhaps just fiction. But of course God knows about them all; if only he could control the people those flashing dots represented! But of course He had given humans free will, so it was now out of his hands. If only Adam hadn't eaten that apple/pomegranate/whatever! But I digress.

Wait a minute – another, different coloured, flashing dot has just appeared on the edge of God's larger/smaller scale map! Who can this be? S/he referred to his/her very complicated colour coding chart. Ah, you are of course there before me, dear reader: it is none other than the vibrant green beacon representing one Phaedra Jenkins, onetime Green activist, now almost penniless would-be heroine. Shall we see what she is doing? In the words of a positive acting improvisation game, 'Yes, let's!'

Phaedra had spent the three-hour flight from London in a state of extreme agitation, and not just because she had sworn many years ago never to fly again, in the cause of reduced carbon emissions. She was willing the bloody thing to go faster, no matter how much extra fuel it might use in the process. Principles were all very well, but when it came to reality – well, there's always an exception to the rules, isn't there? She noticed that the flight, which was half empty, contained a high proportion of very clean-shaven men, some very recently de-bearded, judging by the extreme whiteness of skin exhibited where luxurious facial growth would once have been. Also several men sporting very black hair did not seem to have gone to the bother of dyeing their white eyebrows as well, giving a very artificial reverse Alistair Darling-type look. Flashing reindeer antlers were strewn over the central aisle, once worn by jolly cabin staff; the recorded announcement of 'Hello everybody, welcome to Santa Airlines! Our flight to Lapland, the home of…' was belatedly cut off in its prime, and the captain proceeded to give very routine reports, with never a mention of snow, Christmas or Lapland. The cabin staff appeared to be getting slowly pissed throughout the journey.

On arrival in Rovaniemi, Phaedra saw the last of the 'Elves' offering 'sanctuary' to many of the new arrivals; several seemed to take it, kneeling and kissing the ground of their new-found haven. No one asked her anything, which was a relief; she thought the British police might have alerted their Finnish counterparts. Again, she did not notice 'Elves' surreptitiously talking into small radios after she passed. She had no idea how far Kemi was from here; in fact, that was all she could remember of the name, never having taken much notice of it 10 years ago. And she was not even sure of that. So she quickly took €100 out of a cashpoint, hoping that would be enough in this apparently expensive Scandinavian country, and went out into the bitter cold.

Shit! She had not expected it to be that bad. Unlike the professional that was Terence, she had not come equipped for the conditions, in any way. She shuffled her way to the nearest taxi rank. There was only one.

'Can you take me to Kemi?' she asked the swarthy driver, expecting he could speak English, in the neo-colonial way she purported to despise.

'Kemi?' the man replied, with what she interpreted as a questioning tone in his voice.

'Yes, it's Kemi-something. I don't know; there's a lake there. You know, big water?' and she made an expansive gesture with her hands.

The man looked at her as if she was an imbecile; but maybe that was a cultural thing, she reasoned.

'Kemi – *something*?' he repeated, making the same expansive gesture.

'Yes, Kemi – whatsit! Are there lots of Kemis around here? The one beside the lake.'

'Kemi - *whatsit*?' he again repeated, this time sans expansive gesture.

'Yes, Kemi – bloody something or other! I'm sure it's near here – it has to be!'

'Kemi – *bloodysomethingorother*?' the oaf repeated again, this time including the expansive gesture *and* looking at her as if she were an imbecile. Phaedra decided this could not be excused on cultural grounds; either he *was* an oaf, or he was taking the piss because she was a woman.

She was about to explode and make the situation much, much worse – when a voice spoke up from behind her: 'Stop fucking around and take her to Kemijarvi, Olavi! She hass urgent business zere.' Phaedra spun round – to see a girl dressed in green, with red cap, pointy ears and red make-up. She recognised her as one of the Santa Sanctuary welcoming committee.

'He vass just pissing about wiz you, Phaedra. Zese vankers are easily amused, and haff lots of time to kill.'

'Thanks – how did you know—'

'Just hurry up and get in ze car, sveetheart; ve elwes know lots off sings. Off you go. Good luck! And Olavi – ze qvickest route, please!'

And with that she opened the car door and thrust Phaedra on to the fake fur-covered seat. Olavi shrugged his shoulders, and moved off from the kerb. 'Fucking bossy elwes – sink zey rule the bloody place! Not like ze old days – ze gnomes were on top zen. So: Loch Kemijarvi is it?'

Phaedra was by this time too nonplussed to say much at all. What kind of place had she stumbled into? She sat back and watched the snow-covered pines and frozen lakes zoom past in the gathering gloom, marvelling at the ability of Finnish drivers to happily drive on roads covered by what looked like feet of compacted snow. And not a casteye to be seen. Zey must all be indoors, keeping varm.

18

The dots on God's map were now getting very close indeed. If he was a betting being he might have put a few qvid on which ones would actually collide first, with a heavenly bookie. Most of them had gone in the other direction, however. If only he could interfere in human affairs! But that would be bad, he reflected; a bit like fixing a race. And that was the main reason most bookies had ended up in the Other Place. And I don't mean Cambridge.

Barry looked at the frozen lake from the snow-covered shoreline. The sky immediately above the pine forest glowed red, from the recently set sun, which had only just peeked over the horizon anyway. In less than an hour it would be completely dark, although last night he had noticed that the moon was fairly full, and the exhibition of stars in this area of low light pollution was amazing. This was, as far as he could remember, the exact place and exact time he had stood, exactly 10 years ago, waiting for Phaedra to appear. The idea that she might not arrive had never crossed his mind; she had said she would. And they were in love. What reason could there be for her not to meet him on Christmas Eve in Lapland? The betrayal, the disappointment, still hurt him now. For God's sake get over it man! You can't spend the rest of your life in some kind of post-disappointment trauma!

It was probably more about what happened next that had affected him, rather than the sadness of the actual moment: the years of wanting to get back together again, getting back together – sort of, then not; seeing her all the time, and she constantly saying she 'didn't know' if she wanted to be with him or not; the jealous rages he got into seeing her flirt with other men, which was an integral part of her character; she being angry with him for that: 'jealousy is a negative feeling'. He knew, he knew! Totally counter-productive, but he could not help it; it ate away at his insides like a virulent cancer. He became something he had never been before: completely miserable, depressed, obsessed. The nights of frustration when she let him sleep with her, and 'cuddle' but not have sex; hours and hours of unsatisfied erections. Because he always found her incredibly sexy – she should have been chuffed. Would not even give him a hand or blow job, the bitch. Was she deliberately trying to fuck with his head? Because by God she succeeded!

The intervening Swedish years, five of them, had certainly helped; but he had had no romance at all in that time, despite a couple of offers. Sven just could not understand; thought he must be gay. The obvious riposte. But he just did not feel like he could give any kind of affection;

he was emotionally on life support, if not actually dead. So now here he was, back again, at the exact spot where his decline had started, 10 years ago, to the hour. He remembered how pleased with himself he had been about the snow heart he had constructed; she would love that. How many men would be so publicly soppy for their babe? But she never saw it, only the photos, and even then the first thing she had commented on was the back-to-front J. What a cow! Why had he been so completely obsessed? That level of absorption had never happened to him before, not even with football. She was 11 years younger than him, which appeals to a man's ego; she was a unique, complicated, contradictory, complex, damaged character; she had beautiful big blue eyes, full red lips, and the loudest orgasms he had ever had the pleasure of being involved with. The long, sensuous, incredibly tactile lead-up to their sex sessions were almost as orgasmic as the act itself; electricity seemed to flow between them when skin softly touched skin. Yes, there were reasons enough there to generate obsession in a man at midlife crisis time. Phaedra *was* his midlife crisis.

All these thoughts ran through Barry's head as he stepped on to the ice. He remembered how nervous he had been about walking on it back then, thinking of it cracking, and that scene from *The Omen* (*II?*); till he had seen a car drive across. From the tyre tracks visible near him now, global warming had not precluded that from happening yet. Maybe Phaedra would finally turn up? A ridiculous thought, but he knew how important symbols, omens and rituals were to her, with her hotchpotch of pagan/Buddhist/humanist views. This was a sort-of cleansing ritual for him; so it was not beyond the bounds of possibility that she might now arrive, 10 years after the seminal event that had had such a negative impact on both their lives, and exorcise the bad karma which had resulted.

He passed several skidoos 'parked' on the edge of the ice; a great method of transport in winter, much used by the locals. And such was their native trust, most were not even locked. The Finns were indeed a good people, he thought; could teach us a thing or two about how a society ought to run. But those long, long winter nights, with only a few hours of twilight, month after month; his brief exposure to it had caused feelings of claustrophobia, and he could well understand the high suicide rate in this part of the world. Where he lived in Sweden was much further south, about the latitude of northern Scotland, so it was not so bad. Good thing he was not living here during the worst times with P.; he doubted if either of them would have survived. How very Romeo and Juliet, the suppressed actor within him thought. He walked slowly towards the centre of the lake, full of melancholia.

Terence had let his eyes adjust to the even dimmer light in the Viisiiko Pub, then strode up to the bar. It was warm, loud and murky in the 'pub'; his extremities soon warmed up. Though inexperienced in pub/bar culture, he had the common sense to know that purchasing at least one drink was the usual trade-off for the warmth and comfort offered by such establishments. He did not particularly want to talk to anyone; small talk was not his thing. Conversation in general was not his thing. But he needed a bit of time to warm up thoroughly, and think about what he would do if he did not find Barry, which was now looking increasingly likely. Had he been foolish to follow that idiot Gerald's advice? Well, he would have paid for it by now, the 'Santa Cull' he had drunk would have caused a lingering, agonising death in a few hours. And Terence was fairly sure the decrepit ex-Santa would have quaffed the contents of the bottle as soon as he could.

He saw an empty stool by the bar; all the other tables seemed to be occupied by men and women, of all ages, in various stages of drunkenness, mostly fairly advanced. Big jackets, fur hats and checked shirts were the predominant fashion; off-key singing of Finnish folk songs the occasional accessory. He sat on the stool, and ordered a Coke. The young barman looked at him strangely, shrugged, and went off to do his command. A brown bottle of something Terence had never seen before stood on the bar in front of him, empty. A naturally curious person, and also thinking he might need a subject for conversation with this barman, he picked it up and smelled it. Bananas! How very strange; it looked like a beer bottle. Here indeed was a subject for conversation.

'Excuse me, what is that?' he asked the barman, when he had returned with the Coke, on ice. *How very unnecessary*, thought T.

'That is Sahti, one of our national drinks,' the young lad said proudly. 'It is not to everyone's liking, it has an – um – unusual taste. Would you like to try one?'

'Oh, thanks all the same, but no,' said the young English geek. 'Do many people drink it?'

'No, not really these days. But some of you English have a taste for it!'

'Oh really? Why do you say that?'

'Well the guy who drunk that was British, and he was sitting on that same stool a few minutes ago.' The barman happily rested his case, grinning through the straggly beard of youth. The Finns got there before you, Hoxton types!

'Who? What, just now? Who was he? Where did he go?' Terence snapped out of pretend conversation mode, and bristled with alertitude. 'It might be this friend I am looking for,' he added in a calmer vein, in case the barman became suspicious of his over-exuberant reply and clammed up.

'Didn't tell me his name; you British are not very good at giving names. Said he had been a Santa at Soumutunturi ten years ago; that's not far from here. Said he was here to look at something that happened then? Not sure what he meant. He seemed a bit drunk, and a bit sad. No wonder, with all this stuff happening to Santas, hey? Good thing we don't believe in that stuff here so much. His name is Joulupukki anyway, and he lives on a hill north of here. The real one, I mean.' He smiled at the skinny man with the luxurious blond moustache, expecting a look of mutual understanding at his comic comment; but he got what looked like hatred instead.

'Where did he go?' the moustache trembled as it barked the question.

'On to the lake, I think. Hey, that's two euros for the Coke, man…'

But he was speaking to a swinging door.

Phaedra was still watching forests slip by, with the occasional reindeer by the roadside to break the monotony. They, at least, were real; first she had ever seen. Olavi was singing Finnish heavy metal songs, possibly for the same reason. Light was receding.

Barry stopped a few hundred yards from the shore, and looked about him. Snow-covered pine forests on low hills surrounded the entire lake, with only the last/first few houses of Kemijarvi showing any evidence of human presence. In the twilight the white-painted ones seemed to glow pink. You could probably walk through those woods all the way to the Arctic Ocean, he thought, and never meet another human being. Possibly some bears and wolves – now that would be exciting – but no people. The country looked vast, empty and monotonous – depressing really. Just like his soul.

Strange, low noises were emanating from the ice somewhere; same as 10 years ago. As then, he wondered what caused them. It was a bit unsettling, not knowing what it was. He assumed water must be flowing in and out of the lake, under the ice; he had been told that only four inches' thickness was required to take the weight of a car. The natural sceptic within him hoped for a few more, just to be on the safe side. Maybe those noises had something to do with sub-surface currents? The thought of a huge crack appearing between him and the shore was not appealing.

He was now around the same spot where he had made the heart last time. Of course there was no sign of it, 10 cycles of freezing and thawing having elapsed since then; but it had probably lasted till about May 2004, unless further snowfalls obliterated it. Locals must have wondered who BM and PT/J were, he imagined; the heart with arrow through it was a fairly universal symbol, he assumed. Symbols, symbols! So very Phaedra. But hers would have included pentagrams and all sorts of arcane quasi-pagan nonsense. The little light remaining in the sky was a fiery orangey-red, low on the horizon where the sun had given up the unequal struggle for another day. Looking up, Barry realised that it was in fact a full moon tonight, or as near as dammit, whatever that means. And twinkling stars were multiplying with every glance. The snowy wastes seemed almost to glow, while the dark forests became darker.

But wait a minute – the 'glowing' quality of the ice on the lake, from the angle he was now looking at it, seemed to reveal an enormous heart shape in the frozen snow! No; he must be imagining it. Too much Sahti, turning his brain to banana mush. He shook his head to clear it, and looked again. Yes, there it was, unmistakable, and clearer than ever now: a huge heart, in almost exactly the same place he had made it 10 years ago! Impossible: a coincidence of nature, freak crack patterns. And, even more coincidentally – were those not letters he could see? No, surely not, this was way too weird; but no amount of head-clearing could change what he saw. The lake must have thawed since then, it did every year; so how the hell could that still be there? Ah, yes, a logical answer: other people must do the same thing, maybe even inspired by his 10-year-old template! Yes, that would be it: bold Finnish lovers would announce their troth in the time-honoured manner, on this spot, every year. Barry was rather touched by that, and wondered what letters they would be, if he could only see them properly. But then a flash from the sky momentarily lit up the ice – and in that brief moment he saw 'BM L PJ'. Even the J was the wrong way round. He looked up in complete bemusement, wondering what the flash had been – and saw the beginning of an epic Aurora Borealis display. Things were getting very weird; maybe Phaedra had been right about rituals after all. At this rate she might even turn up.Terence stood at the edge of the ice, beside the skidoos. He could see the silhouette of a man on the lake, a few hundred yards from the shoreline. There was no one else about; no one to witness this final showdown.

Terence felt a twinge of disappointment. He was not absolutely certain at this stage that the silhouette belonged to the man for whom he was searching, but he strongly suspected it did. And he would soon find out. He put his right hand into the bag he held with his left and stepped purposefully on to the frozen surface, heading directly towards the dark form which appeared to be bending down over the ice. The last orange was turning to yellow and fading from the sky, but the moon was bright and stars in their millions were coming out of hiding. He was so intent on his prey that he did not even notice the start of the Aurora display, but tugged off his moustache and threw it contemptuously away as he strode forward. There was no need for disguises now; the pathetic failed actor would be destroyed by the kind of skinny, spotty geek he probably despised.

Something made Barry look up, towards the shore; he saw a human form there, and for one genuinely heart-stopping moment he thought it actually was Her. His heart leapt within him; shit, he still loved her! He still flipping loved her! His reaction shocked him. So he had not moved on at all! Come all this way and done all this to absolutely no avail! The revelation was devastating. What the hell was he doing here then?

Terence saw that the silhouette – which he was certain was a man, and almost certainly the one he most wanted – was looking intently at the ice. Despite the gloom, he saw him noticeably stiffen, as if he had noticed something. But so far he did not seem to have noticed Terence in the gloaming. The selective assassin knew the 'heart in the snow' story, and wondered if that had anything to do with his quarry's reactions. Then the Most Evil One looked up and turned towards him, and Terence knew he had been spotted. That was OK though, there was no way he could know that Terence had tracked him here; no one seemed to know where the hell Barry was. It was only the most amazingly lucky shot in the dark that had brought them together in this place and at this exact time. Almost enough to make one believe in God, or some sort of Fate, he mused, walking slowly and purposefully towards the unsuspecting tree surgeon. But inside, his heart was beginning to race, excitement he was unable to fully control mounting; this was it. Oh, how he would enjoy it.

Meanwhile, the real God was actually bemoaning Fate; he would've put heavenly shekels on Phaedra's green light colliding with Barry's blue first, in a happy-ending scenario, which he generally favoured. But the avenging red of Terence was just about to merge with the blue on his big map, and a purple patch would inevitably ensue, for purely colour reasons if nothing else.

Phaedra's green was not far off, however, and moving faster than the other two. She was currently crossing the Kemijarvi city limits. There's a song in there somewhere, Finns.

Barry almost immediately saw that the person on the ice was not his ex: completely wrong shape, size and movements. Strange how clearly he remembered hers, after all these years. But then maybe not; physically he had adored her. He felt a flush of disappointment, but also of relief. He did not know what he would have done if it had indeed been the voluptuous actor/activist. As for who it actually was – he was not concerned; though the man, tall and skinny by the look of him, dressed in a long trench-coat-type thing, and carrying a small holdall, seemed to be heading directly towards him, as if he had something to say. Barry did not want to be interrupted from his musings, but he stood and waited as the man advanced towards him, ready to be engaged in conversation. He hoped the intruder spoke English, or at least Swedish; Finnish is a notoriously difficult language to learn.

Terence said nothing till he was about five metres from Barry, but kept his eyes locked on the older man, his right hand in his small brown holdall. He was trying to make out the features of the failed actor, in this dim light. He saw straggly fair hair under a black Astrakhan hat, which gave him a vaguely Russian look. His bulky jacket was of course checked, like all the natives, this one being a red tartan; his trousers equally bulky, with an Army Surplus look about them. His big boots looked similarly military, or ex-military. Terence could not see his face, what light there remained coming from behind the latter-day tree surgeon; but his whole body was in an alert, expectant, listening pose.

But not alert enough to save his life, he thought; *the fool will have no idea what is coming next.* A warm, expectant feeling consumed his body; he realised he was actually smiling.

On God's map, the red and blue lights collided, and remained flashing purple. He sighed; nothing he could do about it now.

19

Barry watched the younger man approach; he could see the specs, the long grey greatcoat, the Russian-style flapped fur hat, the big leather boots, a bit like jackboots. Despite the bulky coat he could tell that the visitor was fairly skinny, and much younger than himself. He did not look Finnish or Swedish, for some reason, and seemed intent on reaching Barry without greeting him. A Scandinavian would have spoken or waved by now.

'Terve,' Barry said, in what he hoped was a friendly manner, when the lad finally stopped about five yards from him. It was one of the few Finnish words he had picked up, an informal 'hello'.

'Are you trying to say "hello", *Barry*?' the stranger said, in a slightly strangled voice, with a hint of West Country in there.

'Yeah, it's Finnish – do I know you?' Barry replied, more than a hint of surprise in his voice.

'Probably not, Barry, but I think I know you.' There was something slightly odd in the skinny man's tone, Barry thought; an old friend would surely have greeted him more warmly, especially in this odd, David-Livingstone-I-presume-esque situation. But not odd enough to make him worry.

'So who are you then? You're British, aren't you? Did I meet you when I was here before?'

He could not have asked a more apt question, albeit accidentally. Barry could see the man nodding his head slowly.

'That's right, Barry McLeod, you did. Ten years ago, to be precise; but you probably don't remember.'

'Ten years ago? When I was Santa at Soumu? You weren't working there with me, were you? I'm afraid I don't remember you.'

'I didn't think you would. But I remember you all right. You gave me this,' and Terence finally withdrew his right hand from his brown bag – to produce what looked to Barry like a big toy handgun – plastic, as far as he could make out.

'Oh – so you were one of the kids who came to see me, when I was Santa? Well I wouldn't recognise you now, that was ten years ago, you would just have been a little boy then!'

Barry's mind was now beginning to wonder what the hell was happening here; this was way out of the ordinary. Surely this man/kid had not come just to say 'thanks'? Or return the present because it had broken? A modicum of concern surfaced.

'Eleven years old, to be precise,' the geeky youth replied. 'My grandparents took me. They're dead now.' Something about his last words unsettled Barry; his hands became fists, ready for whatever action might be required.

'Right. So why do you want to see me then? How did you find me?'

'Why do I want to see you then? Why do I want to see you? Mmm… tell me Barry, when you were "playing" Santa, did you ever wonder what effect it had on the kids who came to see you?'

'Yes, I did: I hope I was convincing. I hope they thought they had met the real Santa.'

'Yes, very professional I'm sure you were, Barry. Pity that professionalism didn't help you in the rest of your acting career. You might not've been forced to do this kind of shit. Might've lived a bit longer.'

Alarm bells were now sounding inside Barry's black Astrakhan; but there could be no danger from this skinny young geek, could there? Barry was fit and strong from his tree work; and not averse to a bit of fisticuffs if need be.

'Look, what do you want? Why the hell have you come to find me? How did you find me anyway?' His tone was now very annoyed.

'Never mind how I found you Barry. The fact is, I have. I've been wanting to meet you for ages. I've met a lot of Santas recently, but none of them were you, unfortunately for them.'

The penny finally, belatedly, dropped.

'You're the fucker that's been killing all the Santas. You're the fucking psychopath!'

Terence bowed deeply. 'Terence Wilkinson, destroyer of lies, revenger of wronged children, at your service. Your executioner, Barry.' The temperature was probably about -17C, but a cold shiver – no, more of a shudder – ran through Barry's entire body at those words. His eyes darted to the toy gun Terence was aiming at him. Terence interpreted his glance in the gloom.

'Yes, this is the very "present" you gave me Barry, all those years ago. The one I had asked for in my letter to Santa, which you had in your hand when I came to see you in your "house"! How could I not believe in you? The reindeer, the huskies, the snow, the right present and the letter I sent – how could I not believe? Even the fucking "Elves" were speaking a foreign language – you told me it was Elfish! You had all the answers! I went back home and believed in you for three more years!'

'Well, so what?' said Barry, genuinely bemused.

'So what? You're asking me so fucking what?' the bespectacled killer spat out. 'I'll tell you so what, you pathetic never-been wanker! Because of you – because you were so fucking convincing in your role as Father Christmas – got to be the best role you have ever played – I went home believing absolutely in you. My "peers", if you can call them that, had stopped believing when they were nine or ten; but because I had *seen* you, with my own eyes, in your home in Lapland, and you had given me the present I wanted, I *knew* you were real, and they were all wrong. Of course my parents,' the word spat out, like a horrible-tasting medicine, 'joined in with the lie, wanting to keep me a child as long as they could. But my life became hell at school: constant ridicule because of my belief and "childishness", ostracism, bullying. I became lonely and friendless, losing the ability to interact with others, because I knew they would hurt me, physically or mentally. Teachers did not help me, parents did not know – I was an only child, no big brother to back me up. School became hell, I avoided it as much as I could, hanging around amusement arcades, the traditional thing for truants to do. And certain men took advantage of me, also fairly traditional for truants. Then when I found out the truth, that none of it had been real…'

'Look, I'm really, really sorry Terence; it sounds…terrible. Terrible. But we had no idea that what we were doing would lead to things like that!' Berry interjected, feeling genuinely sorry for Terence. 'But that's no reason to go round killing people who have been Santa at some point!'

'But it's not just me, is it? The same thing has been happening to people like me for years and years – all over the world! Santa Claus is the biggest lie in the world; bigger than God, Jesus and the Moon landing now. Everybody buys into it! It supports the entire capitalist consumer society! It has become a religion! Instead of being the Kindest Man in the World, Father Christmas is the most avaricious, the most materialist, the Most Evil Man in the World! And so are his high priests, people like you who pretend to be him!'

Terence had worked himself up into a frenzy; he had wanted to say these things to the man he now knew as Barry McLeod for seven years. He wanted to justify himself to the person most responsible for his subsequent actions. By the flashing lights of the Aurora, which was making curtains of blue, green and purple light in the sky above them, Barry could see the mad gleam in Terence's eyes. But he had heard enough.

'Look, I am really, really sorry about what happened to you Terence – really I am. But you can't blame me for the actions of others. I was just doing my job.'

'Just what the Auschwitz prison guards said,' the geeky youth shot out.

Being compared to Nazi concentration camp guards was too much for Barry. 'I've had enough of this – I'm off. It's getting bloody cold out here. You should hand yourself in to the police, Terence, they're bound to get you in the end anyway,' and he started towards the shore.

'Oh don't go yet, Barry – we have so much to talk about,' the young nutter purred, 'and I have this.' He held up the toy gun.

Barry stopped; this was getting very surreal. Even in this light he could see it was a plastic toy gun.

'The gun I gave you ten years ago? And?'

'Well you see, Barry, in the years since we met I have not been idle. One advantage in having no "real" friends is that one can concentrate on doing things, learning things. The Internet is, as you know, a mine of information. Once I realised what my mission in life was, I set about learning all the things that would help me achieve it: computer hacking, disguises, manufacturing explosives, et cetera. And handgun manufacture. This,' and he waved said gun around, 'may have started life as a toy, but I have subsequently replaced almost every bit of it with real, functioning parts. It is now a working weapon, and, very appropriately, will be the one used to kill you. Now would you like to stay a bit longer, extend your miserable life by a few minutes?'

Barry studied the plastic weapon; his mouth was very dry. Normally he would not have believed a story like that, but with this evil genius anything could be possible. And he was still just far enough away for Barry not to have a chance of grabbing the gun from him.

'I don't believe you,' he said, with little conviction.

'I didn't think you would,' replied the Evil Genius, with a slight smirk. 'I wouldn't, if I didn't know me. But I would like you to know that it definitely works, so that you can be in no doubt that you *are* going to die, for your last few minutes. So…' And with that he pointed the gun at the ice, somewhere around where the heart was – or wasn't – and pulled the trigger.

About 300 yards/280 metres away, Phaedra heard the gunshot. Yes, my loyal readers, she is still here, her green light flashing on the town map of Kemijarvi. I know you have missed her largely comic input into our tale. The town is on a promontory which divides the lake into two parts, Kotajarvi and Patojarvi. After flinging all her spare euros at Olavi, to his chagrin, she jumped out into the cold and darkness. And by fuck it was freezing. He had told her about the town's physical situation; but which bit of the lake would Barry be on? And Terence, if he had got this far? Neither was a certainty; a nagging doubt nagged at the middle of her mind that she could be on the proverbial cold goose chase. All her fairly-strongly held beliefs in Fate, a Greater Power, Gaia, the power of thought, et cetera would be tested to the full now. And it was almost dark; how would she see anything anyway?

The gunshot answered one question; there was someone here with a gun. But as to who, where and why, she was none the wiser. Sound travels well over ice, and the report echoed around the frozen lake, giving no clue as to which part, if any, it came from. She ran to the nearest dark shoreline, tripping and falling in the ankle-deep snow, powdery where it had not been trodden down. It was too dark to see more than a few yards from the shore, so she listened, feet beginning to freeze in her inadequate boots. Nothing but strange moaning, creaking noises, which she hoped were something to do with the ice. The girl began to panic, aided by the fact she was not even sure what the hell she was doing here. The sooner she found out, the better for everyone, especially her extremities. She scrambled the hundred yards or so to the other shoreline.

The dying embers of the set sun, the moonlight and the glorious Aurora Borealis lent a bit more light to Kotajarvi, the southerly of the two lakes, which she now looked intently at. And again, the sense of hearing came to her aid; that same ice which had echoed the gunshot everywhere also brought the sound of two men talking to her. Talking (to her), I mean, not 'talking to her'. But I am sure you got that anyway. Sorry to interrupt the narrative. Where was I? Oh yes: and they were talking English. She could not make out exactly what they were saying, but the tone, the rhythm and the occasional word convinced her it was her native language. And there were two people; to be more precise, two men. And, as she listened intently, frozen ear near to the ice to pick up maximum sound, ignoring the increasing numbness in her hands and fingers – she recognised the unmistakeable sound of her ex-lover's voice. It was, indeed, Barry. She was not too late.

She was about to shout out his name when something stopped her – possibly memories of the vagaries of murder mystery solutions, or spy thrillers she had seen; whatever, she realised that letting Terence know someone was here who knew Barry, and would probably be trying to help him, was not a good idea. But she thought he had a gun, and made the reasonable assumption that they were not shooting wildfowl on that frozen lake. She stepped on to the ice, not caring about the thickness thereof; if it supported Barry and Terence's combined weight, it would support hers. She hoped. She strained her eyes in the direction of the low voices – and one of the brightest flashes of the Aurora revealed a man kneeling on the ice about 200 yards from the shore, with another standing over him, pointing what was probably a gun to his head. Shit.

Terence had forced Barry on to his knees, 'toy' gun pointed at his head. Barry did not want to die in this pathetic position – he did not want to die at all, to be honest – but the longer he could keep Terence talking, and do nothing to annoy him and make him pull that trigger earlier than he intended, the more hope he had of finding some way out of this predicament. He had been mugged at gunpoint in New Orleans when he was only 21, but this was much more serious; his muggers had not really wanted to kill him, but this psychopath did. It was just a question of when. And there seemed to be nothing Terence wanted in exchange from Barry's life, as opposed to the muggers. They got $17; Terence would get satisfaction beyond worldly wealth. And he had already intimated that he wanted the ex-actor to die slowly and painfully. Barry's body was flooded with adrenaline, eradicating all feelings of cold; he knew his knees would be freezing up on the solid ice, but could not feel that at all. Everything seemed to be happening in slow motion, through a bit of a haze, and almost to someone else, whom he was looking down upon. But other things he noticed with crystal clarity: the flashing lights of the Aurora overhead; the heart shape in the ice (he was in the middle of it, coincidentally; Terence did not appear to have noticed it); the moonlight reflecting from the brass eyelets of Terence's boots.

'This is where your "girlfriend" didn't turn up, wasn't it?' the Killer Geek mocked. 'Tell me all about it. Go on, relive the pain! How appropriate that you are going to die in the same place. Exactly ten years later. Almost makes you want to believe in fate, doesn't it, Bazza? You are probably already praying to some kind of God! Go on, pray away; but tell me how it felt to be betrayed first.' Terence had now replaced God in Barry's narrowing world; he was right on all counts, and held the power of life and death over him. Barry did in fact believe in some kind of over-arching deity, but right now his mind was more preoccupied with trying to think his way out of this situation. It always happened in thrillers; could it occur in real life?

'Don't call me Bazza, Terry – I hate it. At least allow me that dignity.' 'Bazza Bazza Bazza Bazza Bazza!' Terence's response was pure childishness; he had never really grown up, Barry thought. His parents had won in the end! But what a way to win. Was there any way he could use this childishness against the Santa Slayer?

'Terry Terry Terry Terry Terry!' he replied, hoping his enemy also disliked the shortened form of his name. It would buy him a few more seconds, if nothing else. 'What nickname did they give you at school for still believing in Santa?' He was on dangerous ground; an irate Terence might just pull the trigger early. Or he might get him so angry he made a mistake…that's how it happened in books, anyway.

He was right on one assumption – it made Terence angry. Tears sprang into his eyes; not that Barry could see them. He spoke through gritted teeth, in an undertone: 'Fuck you, *Santa*!'

Then he shot Barry in the leg.

Unnoticed by anyone, dark figures began to emerge from the forests, and move slowly on to the ice.

20

Phaedra heard the shot; it seemed loud enough for the whole world to hear. She also heard Barry's scream/groan. She knew it was his voice; she had no idea what had just happened, but it could not be good. She had to get out there immediately and help him; but how? Then she saw the skidoos.

Phaedra did not like driving cars much, as we know; but her motorbiking days, though long ago now, came flooding back as she looked at the similar controls on the ski-assisted vehicles in the murky twilight. She remembered Barry saying how universal they were in these parts, and how their owners often left the keys in the ignition when they 'parked' them, Finland being a very trusting society. It was a straw, and she clutched at it. She leaped on to the nearest one, which luckily for her was facing in the right direction, towards the centre of the lake. The keys were obvious, the same place as on a bike. With left hand on the 'handlebar', fingers freezing inside the thin mitten, she turned the keys clockwise.

The Swedish Aktiv 'Grizzly' engine roared into life first time; bloody reliable these Swedes, viz. Volvos and IKEA. And Abba, of course. A quick experiment with the handlebars ascertained which was the throttle and which the gear control; Phaedra pointed the front ski at where she thought the shot had come from, switched a prominent switch beside the speedometer (?) on – and illuminated 300 yards of ice in front of her.

To reveal a literally heart-stopping sight. The men were just dark forms against the glistening ice, but it was bloody obvious what was happening. The figure she assumed was her Barry was writhing about on the ice, gripping his leg; 'Terence' was standing over him, pointing what must be his gun at the wounded man. Even from there she could see large cracks in the ice, where the bullets had pierced. One must have gone right through Barry's left leg, the one that had once been broken. What an unlucky limb. Secrecy had now been abandoned; both men must have heard the engine starting, and realised that they had been spotted, when the headlight lit them up. She hoped they could not be certain they had been spotted, especially Terence; to conceal her intentions as much as possible she switched off the headlight, having pointed the vehicle at the struggling pair, and opened the throttle as much as she fucking well could.

***

Dark figures continued to advance towards the centre of the lake.

***

The noise of the skidoo engine starting was heard by the men in question, though somewhat masked by Barry's groaning, and Terence's shouting at him. The sudden illumination by the headlight momentarily blinded them;

when it was turned off Barry made a lunge at where Terence's leg had been. But his enemy anticipated that, and stepped further away.

'Still hoping you can get out of this alive, *Santa Baby*?' he roared at his prostrate victim. 'Hoping some bloke on a skidoo is gonna come to your rescue, like in a Bond film? That's the kind of thing you should have done, instead of this fucking Santa shit! Who do you think it could be? Your fucking *girlfriend*, finally turning up, ten years late? What was her stupid name, 'Fanny' or something? Well it's not her, you stupid tosser – nothing can save you now. Listen, he's not even coming this way. No one can see or even hear us. Let me tell you what I am going to do with you...'

Phaedra was fucking freezing in the Arctic darkness, wind chill from the speeding machine making things worse. She was losing feeling in fingers and toes. Her hands were hardly responding to her brain's commands. But she felt elated, excited beyond belief, adrenaline coursing through her entire body, negating all feelings of cold. Fuck orgasms; this was the real thing! She was going to save Barry, make up for all the years she had abused him, and kill this cunt Terence, who had destroyed her beloved Christmas. But the adrenaline also seemed to make her brain sharper; she deliberately aimed the roaring machine 30-odd degrees away from her target, hoping it might make Terence think she was not heading towards them, and gain a few precious seconds of surprise when she finally turned towards them. She had not even seen this manoeuvre in a film; she made it up herself.

Barry's surge of hope when he had heard the skidoo start up, and seen the headlight pick them out, slumped when he heard it turn away. Shit!

181

The rider had not noticed them after all! All hope was pretty much gone now; he could not do much with his wounded leg, and Terence kept just out of his reach. His Internet research on prisoner-taking had paid dividends. Pain was just beginning to flow from the wounded limb, and it would only get worse. But he still could not bear to beg for mercy; he did not want his last few seconds in this life to be spent grovelling to a spotty, weedy geek, albeit a psychopathic one with a gun. So he used Terence as his confessor instead.

'Being Santa here fucked up my life as well, you know, Terence. Phaedra, my babe, didn't turn up here on Christmas Eve, as I think you know. We split up when I got back, but it was very messy, and we both had mental breakdowns, of sorts. That's why I escaped to Sweden, to be a tree surgeon, to get away from her. And away from acting! I couldn't stand the shallowness of it any more. So you see, Terence, we have both been damaged by what happened here ten years ago.' It may have been his last desperate throw of the survival dice, but it was also true. To a certain extent they were both victims of the Christmas Cult. Terence much more so, however.

And he knew it.

'Oh boo, hoo, hoo, poor old Bazza! Had to give up being a luvvie, and do a real job instead! How awful for you dahling! How you must have suffered! But not as much as me. But you will now. Let me tell you what I am going to do with you. I have four "rounds", I believe they are called, left in this gun. I will probably use three on your remaining limbs, thus completely incapacitating you, whilst leaving one for "emergencies". I also have here a large hunting knife,' which he now withdrew from his coat. It was exactly as described. 'I purchased it in the hardware store here – they had a large selection, due to all the hunting that goes on in these parts, I should imagine. And you a vegetarian too! How ironic. With this I will cut out your still beating heart – you should be able to see it in my hands for a few seconds before you die, in great agony, naturally. Your brain may stay alive long enough to see me place it on the ice here, making real the metaphor you made ten years ago, when you made that pathetic heart in the snow. The ice will be red with your blood, pumping out of your dying body – the last, and most evil, 'Santa' will have got his just desserts. Your 'Fanny' might even hear about the way it ended, and realise the significance, if your body is discovered before wolves, eagles or other scavengers get to it. She will feel eternally guilty, and probably kill herself.'

'No, she fucking well won't!' Phaedra said to herself. She had taken the skidoo slightly beyond where she estimated the protagonists to be, and slowed the engine down to tick over, hoping they might think she had passed them. In this she had succeeded. She turned it to face where she could hear Terence's voice, and caught his last words. She was not a second too soon. She flicked the light switch on, and opened the throttle as much as she could, almost being thrown off the skidoo by the G-force as she accelerated straight towards the spotty, geeky murderer, with an ear-splitting roar. Her clever manoeuvre also meant the light now shone more fully into his eyes, rather than on the back of his head if she had come directly at the pair from the shore. Shocked, startled and blinded, he turned to face her.

***

Dark figures had now formed a loose circle around the trio, about 50 metres away.

***

Terence had turned at the sound and the light, startled at this unexpected turn of events. He tried to shield his eyes from the blinding headlight with his left hand, and took the gun away from Barry, pointing it as close to the position of the mystery skidoo rider as he could with his right. But, never having studied skidoos in his Internet assassin research, he was unsure exactly where that would be. The racing, roaring machine was almost upon him when Barry lunged forward on the ice, and with a shriek of pain grabbed Terence's foot, and pulled it.

In the split-second before impact Phaedra saw the gun come to bear on her. She instinctively ducked, catching a final glimpse of shock, hatred and then fear on the brightly illuminated face of the skinny murderer; she heard a shot ring out above the roar of the engine, then flung herself sideways on to the ice a millisecond before her steed rammed at full speed into her target.

Barry's grab of Terence's leg, however weak, had been enough to deflect his shot away from the oncoming monster, and the bullet rammed into the now battered ice. He tried to shield his head from the results of the impact, as Terence's body was thrown over him; and the skidoo, knocked on to its side by the impact, began to run around in circles, the edge of one of its caterpillar tracks gripping the frozen ice and snow. The engine continued to roar, with the headlight rotating round the ice like some hellish lighthouse. Phaedra had not used the kill switch cord, which would automatically stop the engine if the driver was thrown off; she knew nothing about that vital health and safety feature.

All three actors in this macabre finale were now lying groaning on the ice, with varying levels of injury, as the roving headlight lit up the scene, almost like a strobe light. If this were a film, it would be shot from above at this point, showing the action taking place within the phantom ice heart shape. Phaedra was the least injured, being merely bruised and battered from her sliding impact with the ice; she stood up as quickly as she could, not knowing the extent of anyone else's abilities.

'Barry! Barry! Is that you? Are you OK?' she yelled, trying to make herself heard above the skidoo engine. At this point in the proceedings she was not absolutely certain who she had saved, and who she had hit; but she would have been bloody surprised if neither of them were Barry or Terence. The man she hoped she had saved had no idea who his saviour was; some local Samaritan or superhero was his current guess. But that voice sounded familiar…he turned to face it, groaning with the pain which had now taken full possession of his leg. The swivelling headlight caught his features on its next circuit, lying on his side on the ice – and Phaedra yelled with joy and relief to see it was in fact the man she hoped it would be – and that he was still alive.

'Barry! It *is* you! Thank fuck you're alive!' and she tried to fling herself on the stricken surgeon (of trees). But ice having the slippery properties it does, and her boots not having the wherewithal to resist those properties, her feet shot from under her, and she crashed heavily on to his wounded leg.

Words and letters cannot accurately describe the noises of extreme pain that emerged from his mouth; so I won't try. I would imagine you can imagine.

'Oh Barry, Barry, I'm so sorry – for everything! Did he shoot you? In your leg? How bad is it?' Words of relief, apology, sadness and distress flowed out of Phaedra's mouth. Her body was still flushed with adrenaline; she had not come down yet.

And still the skidoo rotated on the frozen surface, engine running, headlight swirling, piercing the all-encompassing darkness. The dark figures were just outside its light circle, surrounding the combatants, looking in.

'Phaedr— what you— how did you— *what the fuck is Terence doing?*' Barry managed to gasp through the gritted teeth of pain. The cold and numbness in other parts of his body seemed to have no ameliorating effect on his wounded leg. Phaedra had forgotten about the would-be assassin in her concern for and relief about Barry; with a jolt she remembered the third participant in this scenario, and looked desperately in the direction she had seen him being flung by the impact.

The evil geek had been severely injured in the altercation with the snowmobile; probably many bones broken, including his hip. But, like all evil genii in films and books, he seemed to be intent on fulfilling his dastardly plans, whatever the cost to himself. Phaedra could hardly believe it as the rotating searchlight revealed his attempts to stand up and totter towards them. His gun had been thrown far away by the impact, invisible in the darkness now. But he still had his large hunting knife, and this he was brandishing as he stumbled towards the stricken pair, continuing despite his screams of agony. Full marks for tenacity, thought the relieved heroine. But what could she do now? She had nothing to fight him off with, she could not get Barry away from him, and there was not enough time to try and get back on the skidoo, get it upright, and charge him again. Try and attack him anyway? She had to protect Barry, he was helpless with that wounded leg; but the thought of launching herself at someone with a huge, wicked-looking knife was terrifying. But help came from a completely unexpected, and non-human, quarter.

The din of the still-roaring engine drowned out all other sounds, including the creaks and groans from the ice; without its noise they would have been very noticeable. Barry had felt strong vibrations whilst lying in agony, but, understandably, had other things on his mind. Phaedra had noticed big cracks in the ice whilst advancing on the skidoo, from where Terence's shots had pierced the surface; now, as the nightmarish figure staggered towards them, knife raised, she saw that those cracks had increased and joined up, and water was flowing over the ice. And, preposterously, she realised that those cracks had linked up to form what looked like a heart shape – with the three of them inside. She had no idea why, but that is how it looked in this bizarre light.

'Barry! We've got to get out of here! The ice is going to break!' she shrieked at him, grabbing his coat and trying to pull him away from the advancing lunatic. Her feet slipped all over the ice, Barry cried out in agony, but she had to keep trying. Terence slipped on the oozing water, and crashed down with a savage yell. Then tried to get up again. He didn't say anything, concentrating all his energies on getting to his quarry and achieving his aim. He was feet away now. Then Phaedra noticed that the skidoo headlight was no longer rotating and lighting them up every few seconds, but seemed to be shining directly up into the sky. The ice they were on tilted slightly – then she realised what was happening. The tracks of the skidoo had begun to dig into the ice, no longer making it go round in circles, but digging down into one spot instead; it's weight was tilting the ice slab a bit, on the edge of the 'heart', right on the crack. Terence slipped again, crashing down on to his face; his feet slithered as he tried to regain them, and his efforts to stand only resulted in him sliding nearer to the skidoo, away from them. But Barry was sliding too, in the same direction, unable to stop himself.

'Come on Barry, we've got to get away from this fucking crack!' Phaedra roared at her friend, redoubling her efforts to pull him out of the heart-shaped iceberg. The man in question had also registered what was happening, and, ignoring the pain in his left leg, managed to get some purchase on the ice with his right boot, and with a desperate lunge hurled himself, and her, on to the other side of the widening crack, where he lay screaming and exhausted. Too exhausted to even thank whatever Providence had nudged him in the direction of putting on his boot cleats that morning. God would have a word with him about that when the time came; He liked to be acknowledged for his Timely Interventions. Without their counterbalancing weight, the whole ice heart tilted towards the heavy machine, which now pointed directly into the sky, headlight blazing up at the stars. Terence, with broken bones and hip, had no chance of a similar escape – and slithered inexorably towards the still-rotating caterpillar tracks. His desperate attempts to gain his footing and run the other way made matters worse. Barry and Phaedra watched spellbound, with a mixture of relief, exhaustion, hatred, horror – and finally sympathy, as the man who had made it his life's work to kill one of them was drawn into the cruel rotating metal tracks. Only then did he scream.

Perhaps mercifully, the upward-pointing light could not illuminate what followed, so Barry and Phaedra were spared the visual details; but Terence's screams and exhortations for help resounded across the ice, above the noise of the skidoo engine. They heard the rotating tracks chew up those brass eyelets on his boots, crunch his leg bones, move up to his hips; his screams reached a crescendo; then the pair were showered with a warm liquid, jets of blood could be seen squirting up into the headlight, and he screamed no more. The engine spluttered a few times, then stopped, as the rising water finally inundated it; heavenly silence reigned over the shiny lake. Titanic-like, the heroic snow machine slowly slipped beneath the dark water through the hole it had created, and with it the remains of Terence. Relieved of their weight, the 'ice heart' righted itself. The valiant headlight remained shining up at the moon and stars for a long time, visible through the ice as it slowly sank, until it too was finally extinguished, leaving the Aurora Borealis to display its full glory.

Barry and Phaedra just stared at the scene, completely and utterly spent, physically and emotionally. Barry had so many questions queueing up to be uttered, but right now he just felt enormously grateful to be alive.

'Phaedra, I – thank you. Glad you finally turned up. Even for you this is a record in lateness!' Barry was proud of his laconic wit; the Dunkirk spirit, he liked to think.

'Ve knew she vould turn up in ze end – it vass only a metter of time,' a voice which did not belong to either of them intoned from the surrounding darkness. Their heads shot up – to witness an eerie, and not necessarily benign, sight. They were now surrounded by about twenty dark figures, human-like, standing side by side and looking in on them. They could not see their faces, but the heads in silhouette looked strangely pointed. This was getting too weird even by this day's extreme standards. And then the figures all began to light candles, which shone on to their faces, and revealed – Elves. Or rather, people – to be more accurate, women – dressed as Elves, like those at the airport.

'What the fuck…?' was the obvious response from Phaedra.

'And nice to zee you too, Phaedra. You vere only just in time, vell done. Zat Terence vass a charmer, vassn't he?'

Our exhausted but relieved heroine recognised the voice of the 'Elf' who had helped her at Rovaniemi Airport. 'Oh, it's you! How did you— why did you— I don't understand.' The Elf sighed a sigh of resignation, as if she had had to give the same explanation many times.

'Och, qvestions, qvestions, my dear. But you must haff many, I understand. However, frostbite and loss ov blood will soon become a serious issue for Barry here, so I vill be brief. And of course velcome back Barry, nice to see you again. I won my bet wiz ze ozers, zat it vould be on ze tenz anniversary. Sveden is much too boring for a man like you!'

Barry did not say a word; this had gone up to 11.30 on the surreal clock.

'Ve knew vot happened here ten years ago, my friends; ve saw Barry make ze heart, ve knew you did not turn up, Phaedra. Ve vere ferry annoyed wiz you at ze time, but you haff since been forgiven. Some sings take time to vork zemselves out as intended – you must know zat, Phaedra. So every vinter ve vould come back here and make ze heart, as near to ze original site as dammit. It became a local celebrity. Ze more superstitious said it vass done by witchcraft – maybe zey are right. It vass just a matter off ven ze Fates brought you two back here again – ve hoped it vould be at ze same time!' A chuckle ran through the assembled fairy-tale beings.

'I bet on ten years – zis business wiz Terence vass possibly coincidental, possibly not. But ve knew it vould happen sometime, zat amount off passion could not just die. So ve vaited, looked after ze ozer Santas, tended to ze ice heart. Making it must haff veakened ze ice, and Terence's bullets and ze skidoo caused ze cracks to happen at ze veakest points. A ferry appropriate vay for it all to end, I must say. He could not haff planned it better.'

To say Barry and Phaedra were flabbergasted stretches the meaning of that word almost to breaking point. Barry was the first to speak.

'But why couldn't you have intervened to save us before now, if you could see what was going on? You could have got the police or something.' It seemed a tad ungrateful, but it was a relevant question, under the circumstances.

'Some sings ve are not allowed to interfere wiz, Bazza,' she replied, naughtily.

'Who won't allow you?' he shot back, perplexed. And that's putting it mildly.

'Enough qvestions! I told you I vould be brief. Time to get you to hospital, Barry, and you varmed up, Fanny. Here comes Olavi on his new skidoo, luckily replacing his old von vich is now on ze bottom off ze loch. But it did not die in fain, and vill join ze pantheon of great skidoos. Come on now, chop chop! It iss Christmas Eve, time to get busy.' And it was true; the man who had driven Phaedra from the airport skidded his shiny new machine (if it could have been seen in the darkness, pedants) to a halt, still singing Finnish heavy metal songs; well you would, racing a skidoo across a frozen lake in the dark, wouldn't you? The other 'elves' gently helped Barry get on. The pain from his leg wound was only just bearable, however. It was a large, workman-like vehicle, and there was space for Phaedra as well.

'And I believe Olavi hass a luxurious log cabin in ze voods not far from here zat he vould be delighted to let you both convalesce in. Isn't zat right, Olavi?'

He turned and winked at the pair, luxurious moustache twitching piratically – just like Terence's. Phaedra could not recall him having one in the taxi. Barry and Phaedra felt completely spent now, all adrenaline out of their systems, replaced by cold, pain and exhaustion. Someone telling them what to do and leading them by the hand was exactly what they needed. Olavi opened the throttle, and the machine sped towards the shore. Phaedra looked back at the frozen lake, illuminated by the moon and the spectacular Northern Lights – to see it completely empty, only the outline of the frozen heart breaking the perfection of the glassy surface.

***

A strange shape flew across the moon's bright face.

***

God folded up his map, and put another tick in the 'Happy Endings' column. He smiled; knowing Barry and Phaedra, it would not stay that way forever.